Cold Cuts

A Murder Mystery and Cosmic Comedy

by Marcia Mayo

HATS OFF™

Cold Cuts: A Murder Mystery and Cosmic Comedy

International Standard Book Number:
1-58736-123-x
Library of Congress Control Number:
2002093087

Published by Hats Off Books
610 East Delano Street, Suite 104
Tucson, Arizona 85705 U.S.A.

www.hatsoffbooks.com

For my family and friends

I don't deny that you are throughout the book.
After all, real life is stranger than fiction.

CHAPTER 1

Annabelle

It was that dark, dark time just before dawn, on a night with no moon, no stars. A small house stood forlorn, looking neglected. The shutters needed painting, the shrubs were running rampant, and the wind made the screen door creak as if someone were entering without permission. Inside, a woman slept alone.

Annabelle felt a cramp in her chest and it was difficult to breathe. She panicked; she was being suffocated. Needle-sharp pricks ran up and down her torso.

Then, something else. A noise, a grinding sound. Summoning the courage to open her eyes, she discerned two green orbs illuminating the void.

"Damn it, Stella! It's not even daylight. You know I hate to get up while it's still dark. Just one of the reasons I quit teaching school." Stella's purring shifted into high gear as she made herself more comfortable on Annabelle's stomach, and then changed strategies, extending a hind leg until she looked like half of a trussed-up turkey. Somehow she managed to get her tongue to an extended toenail, happily taking care of her morning ablutions now that her owner was awake. Charlie perked up at the dialogue and cold-nosed Annabelle out of bed and toward the bathroom. No rest for the weary or the stupid enough to adopt the pets of others. Stella Blue and Cosmic Charlie. Cat and Dog. It seemed to Annabelle that all she had to show for raising three kids, mostly by herself, were leftover animals—each named for a Grateful Dead song she'd never heard.

The next few minutes would be complicated—a balancing act that required some diplomacy, putting Charlie out to pee while Stella daintily ate, then letting Charlie back in to finish up what Stella had left behind. Annabelle's animals shared their morning meal as they did all meals, only not at the same time. Stella was meaner but Charlie was bigger and less inclined to consider the consequences of his actions.

Since she was up, Annabelle stopped and looked in the mirror. "Shit." What had made her think she should cut her own hair? She'd thought the haircutting kit, purchased a few days ago at a yard sale and used the previous night in a fit of pique, would make her look like Sharon Stone after good sex, but a red-headed Drew Carey was more what she got. Contemplating her reflection, Annabelle considered, once again, how hard it was to be a woman at fifty, choosing between holding it together a while longer with bailing wire and Max Factor or letting it all hang out and coming to terms with aging and true self.

Finally making her way to the front of her house, the part she used for work, Annabelle noticed the dust fairies capering in the corners and the ailing plants (the only Deadheads currently in residence) in their garishly painted pots. Black Lab and variegated cat hair wafted through the feeble morning light.

Through the years Annabelle had planned how her gallery/studio would ultimately look. This was not it. She'd envisioned a well put together, possibly minimalist, approach to art and artistic temperament—a salon perhaps—a place where art and idea would converge with Democratic cause célèbre. What she hadn't calculated was either place or person. The place was River's End, Georgia and the person was she, Annabelle McGee.

Even though she'd lived in River's End her entire life, Annabelle hadn't taken into account the fact that her home town was not only at the end of a very minor, mostly dried up tributary of the Flint River, but it was also at the end of the road in Southwest Georgia, where she and Jimmy Carter were most likely the only Democrats. Not exactly a Mecca for either artists or liberals. However, when Annabelle was being completely honest, which wasn't very often, thank God, she knew she couldn't sole-ly blame River's End for not allowing her to fulfill her dream, or maybe for changing that dream into a more pragmatic reality. She, Annabelle McGee, was big on big ideas and short on follow through—a dilettante with lots of rhetoric and little execution. Nevertheless, she had a good life at mid life, a bit bohemian for the hinterlands, maybe, but it was all hers and she was happy with it.

Charlie and Stella

HEY CAT, THANKS FOR WAKING MAM UP. I WAS ABOUT TO PEE DOWN MY LEG.

Charles, must you be so profane? And keep it down. I'm fin-ishing my bath.

HEY CAT, WHAT DO YOU THINK ABOUT THAT NEW CAT FOOD? I THINK MAM GOT IT ON SALE. I SURE WISH I COULD HAVE DOG FOOD LIKE OTHER DOGS.

I agree it's sorely lacking. Maybe I need to get sick on the bath mat.

J.B.

"My God, what've you done to your hair?" demanded J.B., Annabelle's neighbor and best friend, as the newly-shorn propri-etor of The Artful Dodger unlocked her front door and placed the "OPEN" sign in her window. The space Annabelle had formerly called her living room was now The Artful Dodger—a name Annabelle considered quite clever. Instead of couch, coffee table, and TV, the space was currently home to framing materials, art supplies, and a large assortment of salvaged junk.

J.B. was short for Johnnie Belinda. The only things Annabelle Lee McGee and J.B. Jones had in common besides age, gender, and locale were being named after tragic literary figures. Friends for close to ten years, Annabelle and J.B. were polar opposites. J.B. was black; Annabelle was white; a warm mocha to cinnamon freckles. J.B was a married Republican; Annabelle a divorced Democrat. J.B. was a pragmatic complement to Annabelle's way out there. J.B. believed in spending money; Annabelle didn't. It was a yin yang thing and it seemed to work.

Annabelle retorted, "I'm trying to get to my essence and hair gets in the way."

"Does looking like an adult female get in the way, too? You look like a cute little boy, only you ain't little and you ain't cute. And the last time I looked, you wasn't a boy." J.B. was in her sassy ghetto-girl mode, which was difficult for her to carry off since she held a Master's Degree in Computer Sciences and was a web designer by profession. And, oh yeah, a Republican.

J.B.'s husband, who was unfortunate enough (especially for a black man) to be named George Jones, was a professor in the Business School at the local community college. Even though Annabelle had to squelch the desire to call him "Possum" or even "Dr. Possum" when she encountered him, George was not a bad guy in spite of being a George Bush-loving, sell-out, Uncle Tom, who never, ever, stooped to ghetto vernacular. In fact, when trying to impress, he was known to assume a British accent, which was incongruous since he hailed from Texas.

George put up with J.B. and Annabelle's friendship and the fact that Annabelle's 1920's era shotgun house next door was decorated a tad on the avant garde side, something Annabelle was sure George suspected would negatively affect the resale value of his very own decorated, and mortgaged to the hilt, Victorian. The only thing that held him back from complaining about Annabelle's part-time commercial use of her house via The Artful Dodger was his basic good nature and the fact that J.B. was, just a yard away, earning a great deal of money (much more than professor George) in a very commercial way herself as her web design business prospered. Besides, Annabelle suspected that George just hoped people would think her house served as the slave quarters for his house. She also suspected that he lived in daily fear that she would, one day, paint it purple.

Back to the hair, or the lack thereof. "What were you thinking?" demanded J.B., whose weekly-done "do" was the epitome of the latest in black coiffure. "That is one bad haircut."

"I was thinking this shearing would not only peel away the layers of hypocritical societal pressures to remain the ingénue and lay me bare to my very essence, but it would also save me a lot of money. I bought the Flowbee at a yard sale." Annabelle attempted a disdainful finger comb of her orange-colored spikes.

"Oh, honey-chile, we have finally gotten to the crux of your absolute essence. I swear, you are the cheapest person I ever met. I thought Democrats were supposed to be big spenders." J.B.'s scarlet-lacquered fingernails picked at non-existent lint on her linen suit.

"We only like spending other people's money." Annabelle tried an affronted look. "God, you sound like Buster." Buster Taylor was Annabelle's ex, the much-maligned father of her grown children. Buster was also the Chief of Police for River's End.

Annabelle continued with an addendum to an old argument, "Speaking of money, how much did that suit cost? I still can't figure out why you insist on dressing up when all you do all day long is sit in front of that stupid computer in your own house?"

J.B. leaned forward and tapped Annabelle on the apex of her flat top. "It all has to do with attitude. I sit there knowing I'm looking good and that knowledge enhances my dealings with my customers."

"Well, I can understand that. I do the same in my business," agreed Annabelle.

J.B. checked out Annabelle's get-up. "Yeah, when you spend your days making chandeliers out of old hubcaps, that certainly calls for a dress-for-success approach, all right. I think a man's Goodwill shirt and a skirt made from old chamois cloths sewn together send just the message you're looking for."

"You know the best thing about buying men's shirts at the Goodwill?" asked Annabelle.

"The price?"

"No, the smell. I only buy the ones that smell good. Eau de Canoe."

"Annabelle, men haven't worn Canoe cologne in thirty years." J.B. gave Annabelle a look that said her neighbor had been way too long without either sex or a real shopping trip, and asked, "Do you have any Diet Coke?"

Charlie and Stella

HEY CAT, WHERE'S MAM?

Up front with J.B.

THE BROWN LADY?

Charles, you are a genuinely artless creature. You couldn't possibly be as stupid as you act.

I'VE GOT AN ITCH.

CHAPTER 2

A Visit from PhaPha

J.B. was just leaving Annabelle's shop when an expensively-dressed blonde breezed in the door. Anticipating the entertainment value of the collision of two disparate universes, similar to a train wreck, J.B. made a u-turn and perched on her regular seat next to the picture-framing counter.

"Annabelle McGee, I swear, you have not changed one bit in thirty years," emoted the blonde, not looking at Annabelle while wiping off the chair next to J.B. with a Kleenex before sitting down.

Checking to make sure that her hair hadn't miraculously rearranged itself into a perky flip (circa 1967), Annabelle gushed back, "Neither have you, PhaPha!" Meaning that her visitor still appeared to be the same shallow, lying, and self-serving bitch she'd always been.

The blonde continued, "And I love the name of your little store. 'The Artful Dodger' is so cute. But I would've thought you were a Braves fan."

Knowing that sometimes there just weren't words small enough, Annabelle interjected, "J.B., this is Phayla Eberhart. PhaPha and I went to high school together."

Annabelle thought back to her high school days when she and Phayla Eberhart had shared nothing other than four years of common time on alternate planes, never finding, or even seeking, mutual ground. Their paths seldom crossed, as Annabelle hung

11

out with the geeky smart kids who covertly made disparaging but witty remarks about the 'in' crowd, which was PhaPha's realm. PhaPha had been the queen of River's End High School, reigning with a diabolical countenance and very little benevolence. PhaPha had been a user, exploiting anyone who could help her get what she wanted. She'd never wanted anything of Annabelle.

Annabelle continued, "J.B. is my neighbor and best friend."

PhaPha looked like she'd entered a new stratosphere, pondering how someone who lived in River's End (or anywhere) could possibly have a black woman for a best friend. "Actually, my last name hasn't been Eberhart for years. You know I married Billy Franklin right out of high school. We've lived in Tallahassee since then. Billy is a banker." She was actually curling her hair around her finger, *still* the ingénue. No cognitive dissonance about aging there in that cerebellum.

"And what do *you* do?" asked J.B. as she too attempted to curl a strand of *her* hair around *her* finger.

"What do I do? Well, I *am* Billy's *wife*, and, every Christmas, I co-chair the Junior League Gala... plus other stuff."

"It's interesting that Gala rhymes with Phayla," mused J.B., employing the same long "a" sound for Gala as Phayla. "Hey, hey, PhaPha. What you got to say say?" Fortunately, no one was paying her any attention.

"So what're you doing in River's End, PhaPha?" Annabelle asked.

"Oh, I was just out drivin', junkin'. I like looking through all the tacky little stores in South Georgia. You never know when you're going to find a really fabulous antique the little store keeper is just too dumb to know the worth of." PhaPha looked disconsolately around Annabelle's shop as her words dribbled out of her syrupy botoxed mouth.

J.B. perked up at what just might turn out to be something worth postponing a web page revision for. She was really getting into this. "Oh land, I jes know what you mean, honey. Dese South Gawja inbred white fokes is jes so stoopid." All she needed was a big gold tooth to prop up her slack jaw.

With a countenance that said, "I still just don't understand Negroes," PhaPha looked directly at Annabelle for the first time. "While I'm here, though, I do have a little painting I picked up in Tallahassee and I was wondering if you'd be willing to sell it for me on consignment."

"Why don't you sell it in Tallahassee?" asked Annabelle, feeling seventeen again, and like PhaPha was engineering a break in front of her in the school lunch line on pizza day.

"Well, because it's a little...I guess you'd call it naïve. I think it might sell better here. How about if I go out to my car and get it?"

Before Annabelle could answer, PhaPha got up and ran out of the door to her fully loaded Expedition, a car obviously equipped expressly for junkin'.

"I wonder what Phayla drives when she's going to her Gala job?" pondered J.B., looking out of the window.

"Like you have room to talk. You with the BMW. Besides, we don't have time for questions. You need to cover up my chandeliers so they won't get spattered with blood and bone matter because I'm getting ready to kick PhaPha's skinny, liposuctioned ass from here to Wal-Mart. I'm gonna remind her we're not seventeen anymore." Annabelle's agitation had the unfortunate effect of flattening her crew cut.

"Wait a minute, Annabelle." said J.B. "Let's look at what she's got. This is the most fun I've had in a long time. I'd hate to see it end prematurely just because of a little bloodshed. And, by the way, don't forget you're a pacifist."

And so, Annabelle and J.B. steeled themselves for the next assault of PhaPha Franklin (née Eberhart) as Annabelle wondered why, after thirty years, the queen wanted a favor.

The Ugly Painting

When PhaPha re-entered the shop (slamming the door behind her), she was carrying a painting encased in the most ornate frame Annabelle had ever seen. Unfortunately, the garish frame was not the worst news. The painting wasn't just naïve, it was ghastly, an acrylic still life featuring an unfortunate assemblage of vegetables better known for their tastiness than for their physical beauty. It got even worse. Rutabaga, cauliflower, zucchini, and turnip, poorly executed to begin with, appeared to have been situated with definite sexual connotation. Annabelle wondered if she, indeed, *had* been too long without sex, as J.B. always told her, or if this was a new genre: bad art and veggies as erotica. Could be a turn-on for someone. She'd have to ask J.B. to look it up on the Internet.

Annabelle, said, "I don't know, PhaPha. I can't imagine anyone around here hanging this over their sofa. Why on earth did you buy it?"

With a look that said, "I can tell you haven't been to New York City lately," PhaPha responded with, "I thought it had a certain something. I have no idea why the artist didn't sign it. Do you think I can get five hundred dollars for it?"

At this point, J.B. choked until Diet Coke spewed out of her nose. Annabelle said, "PhaPha, you're obviously way out of my league. All the pieces in my shop probably don't add up to five hundred dollars. I think you need to take your, er, painting somewhere else." Score one for Annabelle and all the kids who'd ever had to make do with Turkey Tetrazzini after the lunchroom ladies ran out of the pizza the football team always seemed to have on their plates.

It was PhaPha's turn to become agitated. Her eyes darted around the room and her Kleenex started turning into little tissue balls that landed on the floor. Annabelle would've been offended if the tissue detritus had been there all by itself. As it was, however, it just added texture to the dust. "You've got to take it! I need for you to take it. Please Annabelle, for old time's sake. It won't cost you anything and if it sells, you can take thirty percent."

Annabelle was still busy trying to remember what old times she and PhaPha had ever shared, while figuring how far a hundred and fifty dollars would go in a few weeks when the First Methodist Church yard sale was held. That's if some rich, kinky, veggie-starved sex addict came into the shop and bought the painting before that time. Noting the fact that PhaPha looked like her Prozac had bottomed out, she said, "Okay, okay, I'll put it out and see what happens."

PhaPha dug another Kleenex out of her Coach handbag as tears made marked inroads in her Mary Kay. "Oh, Annabelle, thank you. You know, I always wanted to be friends with you in high school, but I guess my volunteer work took up a lot of my time."

"Volunteering to have sex with the entire offensive line *would* take up a lot of time," thought Annabelle, ready to get PhaPha out of the shop before it looked like a hug was in order. "Here, let me write you out a receipt and get your phone number and address in case the painting sells."

"Oh, no need for that," countered PhaPha. "I'll be coming by in a week or so and I'll see then if there've been any takers." She suddenly seemed to be in a big hurry to take her leave.

Handing PhaPha an "Artful Dodger" receipt hurriedly filled out, Annabelle called, "Wait a minute!"

Before Annabelle could finish her thought, Phayla Eberhart Franklin had stuck the receipt in her pocket and was out of the door and into her Expedition.

It looked like Turkey Tetrazzini all over again.

For once in her life, J.B. emulated her namesake. She was mute.

The Smelly Guy

J.B. left just after PhaPha, appearing dazed, and muttering something about getting to her computer so she could make sense of the world. Annabelle spent the rest of the morning framing prints and wondering where she could put PhaPha's atrocity so it wouldn't offend the Baptists. Too bad she didn't have a back room like they did at the video stores. Unable to make a decision, she left it leaning against the counter. No Baptists seemed to be breaking down her door that morning anyway.

At noon, Annabelle closed the shop and headed to the back to forage for food. She was really hungry. Maybe it was all that reminiscing about school lunches. Apparently, Charlie and Stella had food on their minds, too, since they disengaged themselves from Annabelle's bed sheets and made for the kitchen.

"You two certainly missed an exciting morning," said Annabelle, while Stella rubbed and Charlie drooled. "I wish my visitor would've had the chance to meet you," she continued, imagining PhaPha's response to dog saliva and cat hair on her silk pants. Annabelle knew the best thing about talking to animals was that they always acted like you were making perfect sense and they never gave advice (unlike men). These two had also refrained from commenting on her haircut.

Animals all fed, Annabelle put together a great cheese sandwich and headed to her TV for the noon home decorating show on The Learning Channel. To tell the truth, Annabelle was a bit of a television addict, although she felt confident no one knew this, not even J.B. She was relatively open-minded in her TV tastes, watching everything from "Biography" to "Magnum PI" reruns. However, home decorating shows were her favorite and midday was prime time for these secret pleasures, a time she held sacred. She and the TV decorating experts shared a common ideology, although their projects usually turned out to be more attractive than Annabelle's, and they made a hell of a lot more money. One of her favorite TV-inspired projects had been the one where she'd glued torn-up grocery bags to her kitchen wall. Although her final product didn't look exactly like the one on television, Annabelle felt the effect captured her personality quite well. J.B. agreed, but, somehow, managed to make it seem like a bad thing.

Just as she was sitting down with her sandwich, her chips and her pickle, Annabelle heard a noisy vehicle pulling up in front of

The Artful Dodger. Looking out of the window, she saw a truck even older and rustier than hers. "Damn," she swore, knowing there was a good chance she'd miss a decorating tip and a better bet Charlie would get her sandwich.

Although Annabelle talked Charlie into going with her to unlock the front door primarily to keep him away from her lunch, she was glad her trusty watch dog was with her when she set eyes on her customer. The man slouching on her doorstep appeared to have spent at least the last few days in the clothes he was currently wearing. There was a stain on his shirt that was sort of multi-dimensional. Annabelle couldn't decide if the effect had emanated from one or several assaults by food-type matter or whether that matter had been digested first or not. He also had a greasy ponytail trailing down his back. Being a flower child in the '60s, Annabelle still had a soft spot for ponytailed men, even though she currently believed Willie Nelson was the only one left in her age range. However, she preferred the tail to have been washed within the last decade. This guy was pretty gamey.

"You open?" asked the man.

"Yep," said Annabelle, whose typically off-mark business acumen superceded any fear of being ravished by a really smelly man. Besides, she had Charlie the Wonder Dog by her side. The only problem was that, once Charlie had growled a couple of times and sniffed the stranger's crotch, he shivered, cast a baleful, apologetic look at Annabelle, and then slunk to the back as if to find a good cheese sandwich to abate an unpleasant memory.

"What can I help you with?" asked Annabelle, hoping to get rid of the guy in time to catch the Mailbox Segment on her show.

"Just wanna look around," said the weirdo, already in the shop. Maybe she could interest him in a chandelier.

The man wandered around for a minute and then stopped in front of PhaPha's atrocity. "How much for this?"

Expecting her one customer of the day to fall down laughing when she told him the price, Annabelle apologetically offered, "Five hundred dollars?" She felt the need to grimace and smirk to indicate that she knew the amount was ridiculous. Why was she worrying about what this guy thought? Talk about codependency.

"I'll take it," he said, throwing down five one-hundred-dollar bills.

Annabelle recovered her sensibilities quickly enough to grab the money and place it in her cash register. She'd pay the tax. No need to wake this idiot from his stupor with mere details. Writing out a cash receipt, she couldn't help but pry, "Could I ask why you want this particular painting?"

"Oh, I don't know. I just thought it had a certain something," the man said as he walked out the door, ugly painting under his arm.

Annabelle watched as her customer drove away, and then stood looking out of the window for a long time, thinking about taste, and pondering the robustness of the universe. Meanwhile, Charlie jumped on Annabelle's bed, turned around three times, and went to sleep, full of leftover Friskies and a purloined cheese sandwich.

Charlie and Stella

HEY CAT. THAT MAN UP FRONT SMELLED BAD.

He was significantly lacking in taste, too. Did you see that painting he purchased?

THE SANDWICH WAS GOOD, THOUGH.

CHAPTER 3

The Next Day

The next morning when J.B. arrived for visiting hours, she was carrying an amethyst-colored suede jacket. "Annabelle, do you want this? It doesn't fit me anymore."

Annabelle perked up when she saw the jacket, knowing that fit probably wasn't the problem. J.B. couldn't stand to wear a garment for more than a season. "Oh yeah, this is gorgeous. Do you mind if I make it into a purse?"

"Now, why on earth would you want to take a perfectly good jacket and make it into something else, especially a purple pocket book?" asked J.B., raising her voice. "Never mind. Don't tell me. Artistic license or the need to create, some bullshit like that. In your case, it's probably because the purse that you've carried for the last fifteen years has finally sprung a leak and you're too cheap to go buy a new one."

"You got that right," agreed Annabelle, taking no offense, before changing the subject. "J.B., that painting PhaPha left yesterday. Is it my imagination or did it have a definite sexual feel to it?"

"Well, that was one big zucchini," said J.B. "By the way, where is it? Have you hung it over your bed?"

"That's what I'm trying to tell you," interrupted Annabelle, rubbing a knee that appeared to have recently become arthritic. "You aren't going to believe what happened. Yesterday at noon, just as I was sitting down to lunch, I had a customer."

19

"Oh God, I bet that's a dead person, interrupting your TV fix. Even I know better than to do that." said J.B.

"I don't watch much television."

"Right."

"Let me finish what I have to tell you. I swear, there's something funny going on here. This was one nasty-looking guy. I almost didn't let him in," lied Annabelle, feeling no guilt at all. "If I hadn't had Charlie with me, I probably wouldn't have."

J.B. looked at Annabelle as if she were actually being serious.

Annabelle continued, "The long and short of it are that he bought the painting. Didn't even look at anything else. Not even my chandeliers. He just plopped down five hundred-dollar bills and took the painting."

J.B. looked at Annabelle with concern and asked, "Did you forget to charge tax again, Annabelle? I swear, you'll end up doing time for tax evasion."

"I remembered, but didn't want to slow him down. I'll take care of it. I promise," said Annabelle. "But J.B., doesn't this seem strange to you?"

"The only thing that seems strange is your inability to do business and your aversion to making money," argued J.B. "Maybe he's some rich retro-grunge art collector. Remember what PhaPha said—she said that she thought the painting had a certain something."

"That's another strange part," said Annabelle. "When I asked him why he wanted that particular painting, he said almost the same thing, word for word, that PhaPha had said. He said he thought the painting had 'a certain something.' Plus he had Alabama tags."

"Now I *am* getting suspicious," said J.B., looking out of the window as if to ponder how an art aficionado could possibly be from Alabama. As she looked, she spotted a late-model Ford pulling up in front of The Artful Dodger. "Speaking of nasty-looking characters, it looks like your ex is paying you a visit."

Charlie and Stella

HEY CAT. MR. JACK IS HERE. I CAN SEE HIM FROM THE WINDOW.

Buster, Charles. His name is Buster. Where did you get Mr. Jack from?

I LIKE MR. JACK. I LIKE THE WAY HE SMELLS. HE SMELLS LIKE BACON. DO YOU THINK HE HAS ANY GUM?

I hope he doesn't sit in my chair. I think the sun is just in the right place.

Bad News

"Morning, Annabelle. Morning, Belinda," boomed Buster as he shut the door behind him. He refused to call J.B. "J.B." Occasionally he called her Johnnie, just to irritate her, but mostly it was Belinda. "My God, Annabelle, what did you do to your hair? It looks like you're heading to Fort Benning for basic training. You haven't decided to be a dyke, have you?" As usual, Buster's inability to understand anything important was superceded only by his proclivity for saying really stupid things with great enthusiasm.

"Morning, Buster," replied Annabelle, who was actually quite fond of her ex-husband now that she no longer had to live or have sex with him. "To what do we owe this visit?"

"Just a question." Buster hitched up his pants under his sport coat, his pistol adding heft to the girth already fruitlessly suppressed under a copious amount of plaid. It was just as well that he no longer had to wear a uniform. Buster had thickened a bit through the years. But, then again, so had Annabelle.

"Ask away."

"What was Phayla Franklin doing in your store yesterday?" Buster's countenance had changed to serious.

Annabelle and J.B. both sat up and paid attention. Stranger and stranger. Annabelle asked, "How do you know PhaPha was here yesterday?"

"Because a receipt dated yesterday from 'The Artful Dodger' was found in her pocket this morning when she, in turn, was found dead at Food World." A distasteful look passed over Buster's face as he rested at least a part of his formidable girth on the counter and pulled out a small notebook.

"Phayla Franklin dead? At Food World? How could that be?" PhaPha would never have shopped at Food World. "Where? Out in the parking lot?" Annabelle had so many questions she couldn't even worry about what Buster's ass was doing to her counter. She also felt a little guilty about all the bad thoughts she'd had about PhaPha yesterday.

"Nope," answered Buster, his ruddy face turning to puce. "She was found in the deli display case."

"You mean the real one or an old one out back?" asked Annabelle, horrified.

"The real one. She was laid out like a cold salami." Buster shivered at the thought.

"Oh God, that's where I buy my Cajun-spiced roast beef." J.B. looked like she was seriously considering becoming a vegetarian. "This is going to ruin Food World. I'll never be able to shop there again without thinking about this."

Buster gave J.B. a look that said he wished the future of Food World was his only problem. "Well, the word will get out. We're trying to keep it quiet but you know how River's End is. Plus, I've just told the two biggest mouths in South Georgia."

Annabelle and J.B felt the need to defend their honor. They didn't like enough people in River's End to spread much dirt.

Buster paused while he wrote something in his notebook. "Now, back to the original question. What was the corpse doing here yesterday?" Buster wasn't really all that good with serious police work.

"She left me a painting to sell on consignment. I thought it was odd, bringing it all the way here when there are all sorts of galleries in Tallahassee. That's where she said that she lives. Or, I guess I should say, lived."

"That helps. Your receipt was the only identification she had on her. We're trying to get in touch with next of kin. Any idea who that might be?" Buster's little notebook and stub of a pencil seemed like a cliché to Annabelle. He could at least have had a Palm Pilot. After all, it was the twenty-first century. Well, not in River's End. Maybe she could set up a training session for him with J.B., who had all sorts of technological gadgets.

"Billy Franklin, banker husband, Tallahassee. Billy's from here, but I never knew him. He was older than me," Annabelle felt she needed to give Buster some background since he wasn't a local, being an outsider who'd grown up two counties over. "I never knew PhaPha very well either. We sort of ran in different circles." As an afterthought, she said, "PhaPha was her nickname. I think both her parents are dead. Her maiden name was Eberhart. There's a sister somewhere. Let me think." She paused and then said, "Deirdre, Deirdre Eberhart was her sister. They called her DeeDee. She was a couple of years younger."

After a few seconds, J.B. found her voice for the first time in quite a while and said, with just a touch of irony, "PhaPha and DeeDee, the Eberhart girls."

Buster, ignoring J.B. while standing up and looking around the shop, continued, "Back to yesterday. Where's that painting? I probably need to take it with me."

Annabelle looked at Buster and said, "Sit back down and stay tuned for part two. You might want to take that chair over there. Shake off the cushion first. That's Stella's chair."

Alabama Tags

"Shit, Annabelle. You aren't going to tell me *you* killed her, are you?" Buster's frustration was causing his skin color to veer back toward the rosy hues. "Did she say something about your hair?"

"Annabelle did say she was going to kick PhaPha's ass. I heard her," said J.B., her saintly demeanor indicating only her willingness to aid law enforcement in doing its job. "But it couldn't have been because of comments about her hair. If that was the reason, Buster, both you and I'd be cooling our heels over there at Food World." J.B. looked a little uncomfortable with her use of imagery.

Annabelle gave J.B. a look that said her ass might, indeed, be the next one to be kicked, and then turned to Buster. "What was the cause of death? I forgot to ask."

"Can't tell you. We're keeping that under wraps," said Buster, doing his best to look officious.

"Was she naked?" J.B. joined in.

Buster said "No" but started looking slightly green again. Annabelle knew Buster well enough to figure that his reaction was based more on the notion of PhaPha's nakedness compromising all those great cold cuts than from anything having to do with man's inhumanity to man (or wo-man). "She was actually laid out with a kind of reverence, fully clothed, very chaste. It was almost weirder than if it had been kinky or gross. She was holding a sprig of parsley in her hand." With that, he changed the subject, realizing he might've said too much. "Now, where did you say that painting was?"

"I sold it yesterday, not two hours after PhaPha left." said Annabelle. "Buster, it was the strangest thing. PhaPha was asking five hundred dollars for this really horrendous painting, which, of course, I thought would never sell. Then, just a couple of hours later, this creepy looking guy comes in and buys it, no questions asked. He was really rough looking. I wouldn't have let him in if I hadn't had Charlie with me."

Buster looked down at Charlie, lying asleep on the floor, but decided to say nothing to irritate Annabelle since she was being so helpful. Stella sat on the floor, staring a hole in Buster, trying her best to indicate that he was sitting in her chair. Buster didn't understand cats any better than women.

Annabelle continued, "Do you think the man who bought the painting is the one who killed PhaPha?"

"Can't say, but he's worth looking into," said Buster. "I guess it would be too much to ask that he used a credit card."

"Nope, cash," answered Annabelle.

"Did you get his name?" continued Buster.

"Nope," said Annabelle.

Buster put his head down and ran his hands through his still-robust hair. When he looked up, he resembled a Yorkie, his hair sprouting out over his ears. Or maybe, Jack Nicholson in *The Shining*. "Annabelle, why don't you come down to the station? At least maybe we can get a decent description of the guy and we'll run prints on the money he gave you."

"Wait a minute. A hundred and fifty of that money is mine," argued Annabelle.

Buster riveted his gaze on his ex-wife and said, "Annabelle, that money is now evidence, about the only evidence we've got." He hoisted himself and his pants up and started for the door. Stella jumped into her chair, relishing not only the sunlight but also the warmth left by Buster's big old butt.

"Buster," said Annabelle. "Would his tag number help? I wrote it down when he was driving away. He had Alabama tags."

Buster nodded sagely, as if the presence of Alabama tags suddenly made the whole dirty affair make sense.

CHAPTER 4

Annabelle Goes to the Police Station

Annabelle closed The Artful Dodger an hour early and headed with Charlie to the River's End police station. Charlie liked riding in Annabelle's truck and didn't mind one bit waiting while she ran errands. He was well known in town and people would often stop to speak to him when they saw his black head lolling out of the window. Sometimes they'd give him chewing gum, which he immediately swallowed, but Annabelle didn't know about that.

This time, as she bid him goodbye, Annabelle told Charlie to be on the lookout for the smelly mystery man, a job she could tell he was taking seriously since he was already snoring before she had the truck door completely closed.

As she entered the Police Station, Annabelle was greeted by Martha Mason, the department's receptionist/911 operator. Martha was sweet but really stupid. That second trait served her well in her profession in that she never over-thought anything, nor did she take matters into her own hands. She followed the rules to a T because, to tell the truth, she was just too dim-witted for higher-level thinking. While this worked well professionally, it had hindered Martha somewhat socially. She was the most boring and inane person Annabelle had ever met.

"Hey, Annabelle! I like your hair!" greeted Martha.

"Thanks, Martha. I cut it myself," offered Annabelle.

"Oh Law, I would never have the nerve to do anything like that!" Martha did look unnerved at the thought, patting her tightly permed do. "Buster said you'd be coming in. He's waiting for you."

As Annabelle walked down the hall to Buster's office, she was greeted with a couple of double takes from her ex's cohorts. "It's growing out. You should've seen it a month ago when I first cut it," she lied, as they goggled at the notion that what they were seeing on Annabelle's head was augmented by thirty days' growth.

When she opened Buster's office door, Annabelle realized what a toll PhaPha's murder was taking on him. Buster's tenure as Police Chief had primarily been centered on keeping under-aged college students from buying beer and making sure City Council meetings didn't turn ugly.

"Buster, I forgot to tell you. Bobby called and needs a loan. I told him to call his daddy." Annabelle smiled to ease Buster's pain. Although she was cheap and poor, Annabelle was a soft touch when it came to her kids. However, since Buster made a lot more money and had a retirement plan, he bore the brunt of any large monetary assistance for their shared progeny. Buster and Annabelle's three children were scattered all over the continental U.S., having inherited the wanderlust from their mama. They were pretty much self-sufficient but still needed help from time to time.

"Thanks, I sure needed to hear that," said Buster, shaking his head.

"Just trying to take your mind off your other problems," said Annabelle, helpfully.

They spent the next hour audio-taping Buster asking Annabelle questions, which she answered, and Annabelle asking Buster questions, which he didn't.

"Annabelle, I realize you're interested in this case and you feel involved, but the less you know, the better," warned Buster, as he packed up the tape recorder. "This thing is ugly, and I have a feeling, after talking to the deceased's husband, we're getting ready to get a whole lot of assistance from both Tallahassee and Atlanta. You've already been a lot of help. I can't believe you had the presence of mind to write down that guy's tag number."

"Maybe you'll find the perp real soon and this'll all be over," said Annabelle, as she got up to leave.

"Annabelle, have you been watching 'Mannix' reruns again?" asked Buster, as he attempted to pat her butt. He added, "You know, you're still a pretty good-looking woman ... for an over-the-hill dyke."

"Buster, you were always real good with a compliment," coquetted Annabelle as she headed for her truck. She was reminded that stress typically made Buster horny.

Charlie

HEY CAT. I SMELL SOMETHING GOOD. SMELLS LIKE BALONEY. HEY CAT, WHERE ARE YOU? OH YEAH, I'M IN THE TRUCK. WONDER WHY MAM NEVER TAKES CAT IN THE TRUCK. HEY CAT, I SEE THAT PICTURE. THAT ONE YOU SAID WAS SO UGLY. THAT BIG THING IN IT LOOKS LIKE A HOT DOG. WONDER IF THAT'S WHAT SMELLS SO GOOD. WHO IS THAT MAN WITH THE PICTURE? THAT MAN SMELLS GOOD, LIKE MR. JEROME. IS THAT MR. JEROME?

Running Errands

When Annabelle got back to her truck, she looked in the open window and her heart stopped. Charlie was dead, lying on his back. Oh God, the perp had gotten to him because he knew Charlie could sniff him out, pick him out of a lineup with his impressive nose. Just as a scream rose in Annabelle's throat, Charlie opened one eye, sneezed, and wagged his tail without bothering to get up.

"Oh, move over, you damned fool. I swear, you scared me to death!" Just as pets didn't give advice, neither did they take offense. Charlie somehow righted himself and gave Annabelle a nose kiss on the ear, just happy to have her back.

Next on Annabelle's to-do list was to run a few errands. Intent on her need for bread and Friskies, she forgot that Food World was probably "closed until further notice by order of the police," and before she knew it, she was in the parking lot, along with a busload from the Autumn Leaves Retirement Home on their weekly "shopping adventure." The retirees were all huddled around the store entrance, ignoring the yellow tape, which they'd trampled, trying to get the electric door to work. Their driver was still in the bus, ignoring them, busily working on her manicure.

Annabelle, in a rare weak moment, felt the need to intervene. She drove up close so they could hear her and then called out of her window, "Hey, I think they're closed, for remodeling or something." No need to put the senior citizens off cold cuts by telling them the truth, therefore reducing the quality of what was left of their sweet old lives.

As a group, the old folks turned on Annabelle and started a communal bitch about how things like remodeling never happened where they used to live, and no wonder the prices at Food World were so high. For some reason, they seemed to be blaming the messenger.

Annabelle once again realized that she just wasn't meant for the role of Good Samaritan. She quickly pulled out of the parking lot, leaving the angry throng to their driver. As she passed the bus, she gave the driver a small salute, noticing that her own nails could use some work.

Because she still hadn't solved her bread and Friskies problem, Annabelle turned into the Kwik Mart, chagrined by the fact that she would now pay double for her groceries. However, that wasn't the worst news.

As soon as she arrived at the bread aisle, Annabelle knew she'd made a big mistake. Huddled in front of the hot dog buns was a group of women known for their predilection for keeping the River's End gossip network well fed. Annabelle didn't need to think very hard to guess what was first on the agenda for the meeting that was currently in session.

"Oh my God, y'all. Look who's here. It's Annabelle Taylor. I almost didn't recognize you with that haircut." Annabelle couldn't remember if the person addressing her was Marcie, the School Board Chairman's wife, or Nancy, the Real Estate Agent, since they all looked alike to her with their aging sorority girl look. She'd gone to school with a couple of them but that was before they'd morphed into identical faded flowers of the South. The group appeared to have the same hairdresser, who seemed to know just one styling technique; and, obviously, none of them owned a Flowbee.

It did absolutely no good to remind people in River's End that she'd taken back her maiden name. In their minds, she would always be Mrs. Buster Taylor, at least until she snagged some *other* unsuspecting man and took *his* name.

Annabelle tried to grab a loaf and covertly back away but it did no good. "Annabelle, we know you know something about that awful thing that happened to PhaPha Eberhart." The looks on their faces registered something, but Annabelle couldn't find a trace of sympathy or even horror. Then she realized what she was seeing was pure greed, an unbridled desire for information. Next, she expected them to start sucking her neck.

Holding the bread in front of her like a shield, Annabelle grabbed a couple of cans of cat food with her other hand as she stuttered. "Nothing, I know nothing. How would I know anything? Buster and I are barely civil to each other. I'd be the last person he would tell anything to. PhaPha who? I don't know what you're talking about." She knew she was acting like a crazy woman but she didn't care. Besides, if they thought she was insane, they might leave her alone. She grabbed a Bic pen from the display case by the cash register and sort of jabbed it toward the mob and then threw some money on the counter and ran out of the store. She knew she must really be unnerved not to have waited for her change.

As Annabelle got into her truck, she looked back at the Kwik Mart and saw the women inside staring at her. They knew she was lying.

Dinner at J.B.'s

Annabelle was so upset over her near-death experience at the Kwik Mart that she decided to skip her other errands, including stopping by the public library to return books that were due. She was going to have to get hold of herself before she lost total control. Library fines would surely lead to other debaucheries.

When she got home, she noticed several messages on her answering machine, but decided not to check. She just wasn't up to more questions about PhaPha's death. Suddenly, the phone rang and she quaked, then caught herself. Enough hysterics. She answered.

"Annabelle, why don't you come over? George has just opened a bottle of pinot noir and he's cooking up something French, or is it Italian? I can't tell the difference." Thank God! Like Annabelle, J.B. wasn't much of a cook, but George considered himself a real chef. In addition, the Jones' wine selection was an improvement over the big purple jug Annabelle kept in her refrigerator.

"I'll be right there. J.B., you're saving my life. What an afternoon!" Annabelle was close to tears. She was so relieved to be among friends, even if one of them was George Jones, Black Republican.

Leaving Stella and Charlie to defend the store (and the house), Annabelle walked next door, looking forward to the calm that emanated from the order of her neighbors' home. J.B. and George's Victorian was beautifully renovated and perfectly appointed, a serene antithesis to the in-progress chaos that was Annabelle's. Additionally, there was never any dog hair on anything. The Joneses were firm in their no kids, no pets policy.

George opened his heavy, beveled, high-gloss door and handed Annabelle a glass of wine. "I hear you've been cavorting with
murderers, Annabelle."

"Oh God, George. How could something like this happen in
River's End?" asked Annabelle. "I thought we were too far out in
the sticks for murderers. I thought they liked big cities."

J.B. and Annabelle sat talking at the vintage counter the
Joneses had found in an old drugstore and moved into their
kitchen, while George sautéed something. As he worked, George
offered, "Rumor is rampant at the college. Word is the dead
woman's husband had her killed. J.B. told me where they found
her but that information apparently isn't out on the street yet,
thank God." He gave a shudder as he addressed the chicken on
the cutting board.

J.B. chimed in, "Well, that's only a matter of time. Something
that juicy—excuse the pun – isn't going to stay secret. I wonder
what the 'Suffering, Sin, and Gall' will have to say when it comes
out." J.B. was referring to The Southern Sentinel, the local weekly paper that, aside from Garden Club news, relied heavily on
obituaries, arrest reports, and poorly-written yet vehement letters
to the editor for the majority of its four-page bulk. J.B. held a
special disdain for the paper and liked to come up with different
demeaning names for it.

Annabelle said, "Buster won't tell me much and I'm really
glad." The part about her being glad was a lie. "You should've
seen the coven of witches that surrounded me at the Kwik Mart.
It was really scary. And, you know, the murderer could still be
here, and what if it's the loser who bought the painting? He
knows Charlie and I can identify him."

Ignoring the comment about Charlie, George pointed out, "I
think that person, if he's guilty, is as far away from River's End
as possible. But, if you're afraid, why don't you stay here with
us?" George's look of the Christian martyr belied what Annabelle
knew he was really hoping for. He was praying she would turn
down his offer, if for no reason other than the fact that having

Annabelle murdered in his house would be messy and would require yet another costly renovation.

"No, I should be fine, since I have Charlie. Plus, Buster said that he would have someone patrol our street for a couple of days," said Annabelle. As they sat down to eat, both George and J.B. hoped the patrolman Buster sent had more sense (and a better nose) than Charlie. Somehow, they doubted it.

After dinner, Annabelle went back home, the very short hairs on the back of her neck standing on end. She was relieved to find Charlie and Stella where she'd left them, holding up the fort from under the covers. She did take the time to look for weapons, but all she could come up with were a garden spade and an old barbecue fork. Nonetheless, as she placed them under her pillow and kicked the animals out of her bed, she felt empowered. She could just envision the encounter, "Okay, sucker, you have a choice. You want to be tilled or grilled? Raked or baked?"

Not only was she empowered, she was also funny as hell. She just hoped that the smelly guy had a good sense of humor.

With all that said, Annabelle got under the covers and cried herself to sleep, not only for her owns fears but for Phayla Eberhart, whom she had never liked. A while later, Charlie and Stella climbed in with her, offering comfort the only way they knew how.

CHAPTER 5

The Pink Peignoir

The next morning, J.B. was knocking on Annabelle's door before eight o'clock. When she let her in, Annabelle complained, "You know I don't like to get up early. What the hell are you doing?" Even Charlie was not in top form at that hour but perked up nicely when he saw the leftovers George had sent.

"I was worried you might be dead."

"And what were you going to do if I was?" Annabelle asked.

"Clean up your house before the church ladies got here," answered J.B., looking around.

Annabelle smiled at J.B. and offered, "Since you're such a friend, come sit down and have a Diet Coke."

They went into Annabelle's kitchen and sat at the table, after they removed a cat from one chair and magazines from another.

Opening her own Diet Coke, Annabelle said, "J.B., I had trouble sleeping last night." She didn't mention the spade and the barbecue fork under her pillow.

"I guess so," nodded J.B. "I know you'll be happy when this thing is resolved."

"What's really bothering me is that painting. I know people think I'm eccentric, a little flaky, but I know art...and, believe me, that wasn't it. What keeps going through my mind is what would be the purpose of passing on such a grotesque painting? All I can think of is that it had something hidden in it. Something like drugs, or money, or a message, or maybe a key. And the reason it was so awful was because it was easy to identify and also no one else would dare buy it. I think PhaPha was setting me up to be a part of something illegal." Annabelle put the Coke can to her forehead as if to forestall a fever.

J.B. asserted, "If what you say is true, it would make me think PhaPha was a whole lot smarter than she looked, but, then again, she *is* dead." A pause and a look. "Annabelle, I've held off asking this for as long as possible. Why on earth are you wearing a pink peignoir over your t-shirt?"

"You weren't the only one who was worried about me being murdered in my sleep. I wanted to look sexy in case Buster had to come identify my body, but, then I got cold and decided to wear the t-shirt underneath." Annabelle fluffed her attached boa.

"As always, you've put together a good look." It was J.B.'s turn to place the drink can on her forehead.

"Back to the painting. I wish I'd looked at it closer. I think I ought to call Buster and tell him what I suspect," said Annabelle.

"Or, you could ask him to come over and tell him in person. That way he'd have the opportunity to see you in that get up." J.B had finished her liquid breakfast and was headed for the door.

"No, I just think I'll call him," said Annabelle, following J.B. to the front. After a minute, she added, "You know, I really don't want Buster. I just want him to want me."

Charlie and Stella

HEY CAT. I'M GLAD THE BROWN LADY BROUGHT US SOME OF MR. JEROME'S FOOD. IT WAS GOOD.

Charles, her name is J.B. His name is George. Try to get them right, okay? You're really irritating me.

Death on Interstate 75

When Buster came on the line, Annabelle said, in a rush, "Buster, I've been thinking about the guy who bought that painting. I just know he had to be involved with PhaPha in some way. Nobody would've bought that painting for five hundred dollars unless there was something funny going on—"

Buster interrupted, "Annabelle, you're right."

"I am?"

"Yep, it looks like he was definitely involved."

"Did you find him? Is he talking?"

"We found him, but he's not talking."

"Why not? Can't you make him talk? I thought you people had ways to make people talk."

"Annabelle, he's dead."

That stopped Annabelle cold. Revulsion was mixed with the relief that accompanied the knowledge that she could remove the weapons from under her pillow. "What? How? Where?"

Buster hesitated, as if weighing what Annabelle deserved to know against the need to keep certain information privileged. "His truck was found in a wooded area near I-75. He'd been shot."

"That doesn't necessarily mean he was involved in PhaPha's death, does it? It could've just been a coincidence." Annabelle's brain was in overdrive.

"Except that Phayla Eberhart's car was found next to the truck."

Never a great one for organized linear thought, Annabelle was having trouble with how the two deaths could've happened. Either PhaPha shot the greaser, felt so bad about her sin that she crawled into the deli display case at Food World and held her breath until she died; or the greaser killed PhaPha, dragged her to Food World, drove back to I-75, and shot himself. Both of these scenarios sounded like a lot of trouble.

"Buster, could he have killed himself?" asked Annabelle.

"Nope, no gun was found. Wrong distance and angle. All that stuff."

"How about the painting? Was the painting in his truck?"

"No."

"How about in PhaPha's car? Was the painting in PhaPha's car?"

"No. No painting anywhere."

Annabelle was beginning to understand that someone else had to have been involved. She said, "You know, Buster, the rumor at the college is that PhaPha's husband had her killed. You think there's any credence to that?"

Buster sighed. That's all he needed, a bunch of PhDs helping him with his job. He said, "Tell George to leave the police work to us. We can handle things here." Testy, testy. Those professorial types irritated him, always nosing into his business and running for town council. In Buster's mind, real men didn't teach college. "Oh, Annabelle, more bad news."

"What?"

"The five hundred dollars. The bills were counterfeit. Looks like you won't be getting your cut." Buster was actually sorry to give Annabelle that information. He knew how many hubcaps she could've bought with a hundred and fifty dollars. However, he couldn't help but add, "Those bills weren't even very good fakes. Didn't you notice that Ben Franklin looked a hell of a lot like John Belushi?"

Buster sure was a smart-ass for being such a fool.

A Well Thought Out Invitation

In spite of what Buster had said, the River's End Police Department was apparently not deemed capable of handling things by itself. According to The Southern Sentinel, the big boys were being sent in, including the Georgia Bureau of Investigation. The Sentinel's headlines were all about PhaPha. In fact, all of the news was about PhaPha, except for announcements about the Daughters of the Confederacy meeting and the Methodist Yard Sale. From the paper, Annabelle finally gleaned that PhaPha had been strangled. She was a little pissed that Buster hadn't told her that, but she figured he was too stressed out to worry about what he'd told his ex-wife as opposed to what he'd told Eula Eubanks, The Sentinel's ace crime reporter/food editor.

In a thought process that makes sense only to a woman, Annabelle somehow made the connection between being pissed at Buster and deciding to invite him for supper. If she'd thought hard about her motives, she would've concluded that 1) she wanted to see what she could find out about the case, 2) she wanted to see if Buster was still attracted to her, and 3) of most importance, she wanted him to have the opportunity to irritate her enough to remind her of why she'd divorced him. Of course, bypassing the reasoning part, Annabelle simply concluded that she was doing her Christian duty. After all, Buster was tired and stressed and he hadn't had the opportunity to enjoy her cooking for quite a while. If Annabelle had taken the time to delve even more deeply, she might've remembered that, when she was worried or scared, her thoughts returned to Buster and the comfort of having a man to take care of her, which was why motive #3 was crucial.

"God, Annabelle, what did I do to deserve this?" Buster was already working on motive #3. His response to her kind invitation was certainly annoying her.

"Come on, Buster. You used to enjoy my Tuna Surprise," countered Annabelle, trying to keep the whine out of her voice.

"The surprise was that I survived your Tuna Surprise."

"Ha Ha. You can bring a bottle of wine."

"What kind of wine goes with canned tuna?"

"Something expensive."

"Has your hair grown out any?"

"Yeah, I currently look like Farrah Fawcett."

"You got an ass job, too?"

Annabelle could tell this was going to work out well. After she hung up the phone, she got busy cleaning off the table and finding some silverware that hadn't been incorporated into a work of art.

How the Buster-Annabelle Thing Began

Annabelle and Buster had met some thirty years ago on her first morning of student teaching at River's End Elementary School and his inaugural day as a brand new deputy for the River's End Police Department. Annabelle was running late after giving her waist-length red hair one last ironing to try to get it to give up its wave for a more mod look. Buster, in his starched uniform, was ready to begin his professional career, to show his stuff, to write out his first citation as he parked at the corner waiting for someone to speed. Then came Annabelle.

By the time he'd pulled her over and written out the ticket, Buster was lost. Between the undulation of fiery hair cascading down her back and the sun-kissed freckled thighs emanating from her paisley mini-skirt, Annabelle was ripe for picking, a fecund flower bursting with sensual possibilities.

On the other hand, Buster was an interesting antithesis to the skinny, stoned intellectuals Annabelle had hung out with in college. He seemed solid. He *was* solid. In those days, Buster worked out a couple of hours a day with free weights.

Now that college was almost behind her, Annabelle was ready to get on with her life and, even at her jejune age, suspected she would need to align herself with someone who didn't share her artistic temperament, someone with his feet planted on terra firma, someone from good breeding stock. Buster looked like a good bet, what with his manly muscles and big gun. Plus, she really couldn't afford a speeding ticket.

The citation somehow disappeared except for the part with Annabelle's phone number, and the rest was history.

Buster Comes to Dinner

Buster arrived with a bottle of grocery store white zinfandel. Annabelle decided that his choice was actually a compliment, considering what she was feeding him. If the truth be known, she'd spent more time thinking about what to wear than what to cook. She wanted to look good but not needy. In addition, she had to take into account her strong points and current deficits. Her waist and butt were pretty much gone but her legs were still good. She had a great cleavage but her neck was history. She finally decided on a short skirt, a long v-necked sweater and a scarf at her throat. Buster had also apparently thought long and hard about his attire. He was wearing a Lynyrd Skynyrd t-shirt that barely covered his gut and rump-sprung coach's shorts. The man unquestionably had romance on his mind.

"Damn, Annabelle. I didn't know I was supposed to dress up. Is somebody else coming?" How could someone as stupid as Buster slap her in the face with her own subterfuge in his first minute in attendance?

"No, I'm just trying on this outfit in case I have some place important to go later," answered Annabelle.

"Well, it would look good on somebody with hair. I swear, Annabelle, you have such pretty hair. Why do you do such stupid things to it?" This was starting out good. At least he was looking at her.

As they opened the bottle of wine, the talk turned to everyday things, their children, and extended family. Buster poured a glass for each of them as they visited at the table. Charlie, his eyes closed but flickering, kept watch from the kitchen floor. Stella was looking inscrutable from the top of the refrigerator.

"Buster, I think dinner is ready," Annabelle said, her wine glass empty.

"It can't be. I didn't hear the smoke detector go off." Annabelle's bad cooking was a long-standing joke between the two of them, so Annabelle didn't take offense. In fact, she saw Buster's teasing as a form of flirtation.

Dinner, which consisted of the promised Tuna Surprise, green bean casserole, and a jello mold, was a success in that it didn't require much chewing. It was clear that Annabelle associated comfort and womanliness with post World War II three-ingredient recipes. However, Buster, who spent most of his evenings with Madame Stouffer, was happy with three ingredients, which, multiplied by three dishes, equaled nine ingredients. (Cream of mushroom soup was a recurring theme.) As he was spooning up seconds, Annabelle skillfully turned the conversation to the investigation, at least to her part in it.

"Buster, have you thought any more about what I said about the role that painting played in PhaPha's murder?"

"Yeah, I mentioned it to the GBI but they don't seem to think it's important. They believe the husband was behind it. They think he hired the creep to kill her and then balked at the price or something and the whole thing went bad. No idea why she ended up as a deli display."

"Both PhaPha and the smelly guy dead. Both interested in the painting. That seems just too coincidental," Annabelle mused.

"I agree with you that the painting had to be involved, but to tell you the truth, my office just doesn't have the time to pursue it, and the State folks aren't interested, or at least they're acting like they aren't. I don't think they're being very forthcoming with what they know. I hate it that we're going to come off looking so stupid. I just wish I had someone with time enough to check into it." Buster knew not only that he didn't have anyone with enough time, but there wasn't anybody in the River's End Police Department who had sense enough to do much more than park people during the high school football games.

Light bulb! "Buster, I just had an idea. Why don't you let me check around at the art and antique stores between here and Tallahassee? Maybe I could find out something about that painting, where it came from. As bad as it was, it's certainly memorable." Annabelle was getting excited. Art galleries and junk stores were things she understood. In fact, she knew some of the proprietors of the places she'd visit. She was already planning what she would wear. Definitely something arty. A leotard, maybe, with a big scarf tied as a skirt.

Buster shook his head. "I don't know." He hesitated, and was lost. "We'd have to hire you as a consultant or something. Give you a small consultation fee, on a limited basis, of course." He hesitated again, feeling sorry for Annabelle because her big sale of the month (perhaps the year) had turned bogus. He ran his hands through his hair (Jack Nicholson again), and finally said, "Okay. I'll give you one week. A hundred bucks a day and expenses. What are you going to do about your store?" He looked around and realized what a stupid question that was. Just the travel expenses alone would be more than what Annabelle typically brought in. "At least you can use one of your major talents, aggravating the hell out of people. Most folks'll tell you anything just to get rid of you." Buster also considered it a plus that Annabelle and her opinions would be out of town for a few days. He wanted to keep as much of this mess as possible under wraps.

Annabelle smiled, knowing she'd met two of her three goals. Buster had flattered her (not counting the part about her being aggravating), he'd provided some useful information about the case, and had even hired her to find out more. Now, if goal number three could be addressed. She was a little worried about that one. He'd been pretty well behaved tonight. Even helpful. This could be dangerous.

Just then, Buster sat back from the table, picked up a toothpick, belched delicately, and said. "You know, Annabelle, before you leave town, you might want to relieve the pressure a little bit." He winked, the toothpick hanging precariously from the corner of his mouth. "You know what I mean? A little roll in the hay, see if you still remember how. You still got all your parts, don't you?"

BINGO! Three for three.

CHAPTER 6

Travel Plans

❝You're gonna what? Where? With who?❞ J.B. tightened her bottom lip, looking like a black James Cagney.

"I'm going to Tallahassee to investigate PhaPha's murder. Charlie and me. I need for you to feed Stella." For extra credence, Annabelle added, "I've been deputized." That was sort of true.

"Is that what they're calling it now? I suspected you and Buster were getting a little too cozy over here last night. I think I read somewhere that canned tuna is an aphrodisiac. Must be the smell." J.B. flinched, grossing her own self out.

Annabelle was standing with her head in the refrigerator, looking for Diet Cokes. "It wasn't anything like that. Buster is still the same baboon I used to be married to; however, they apparently have leftover money in the department and they could use some extra help. That is, some help other than the GBI. I think Buster is embarrassed that the State people are getting involved. Apparently, they're treating him like the cretin he is."

"You're talking about the father of your children," J.B. reminded Annabelle.

"It's just a good thing that I have all dominant genes," Annabelle countered as she found her quarry in the back of the fridge, behind last night's leftovers.

"Okay, back to your idiotic idea. Why on earth are you thinking of taking that stupid dog?" J.B. had to use the end of a spoon to open her Diet Coke because her nails were newly done.

45

"I'm taking Charlie for companionship and protection," said Annabelle, looking at her companion and protector snoring on the floor.

"Ain't nothing that dog can do I can't do better...except that." J.B. was looking at Charlie, who suddenly had his muzzle entrenched in his groin area, working industriously on his genitals. "And I smell a hell of a lot better."

"What? Are you offering to go with me? What about work? What about George? George will never let you go."

"George will let me go because I keep bringing home cruise brochures. I need a vacation and the only places George ever takes me are academic conferences and that one time we went to that Black Republican's Convention. Plus, when I need a vacation, I tend to lose my sex drive."

Annabelle continued to be impressed with how J.B. managed to look at her marriage as a business arrangement. Supply and demand. Interest and penalty. Bull and Bear Markets. No wonder her CPA husband was so whipped. She did wonder from time to time if J.B.'s marriage could possibly be as good as it looked from next door. Surely George had to have *some* character flaws besides being a Republican.

"What about work? And who'll feed Stella and Charlie?" Annabelle knew J.B. could talk George into feeding the animals, who'd be in hog heaven with leftover coq au vin and lobster bisque, but she wasn't sure if J.B. could leave her computer without Bill Gates' permission.

"This'll give me a chance to get used to my lap top, and who knows what new clients I'll meet in Tallahassee. I'll figure out a way to write off my expenses." J.B. noticed Stella sitting on top of the toaster oven, sending cat hairs drifting over the terrain that was Annabelle's kitchen. She was glad she'd turned down the toaster strudel offer. "And old George will feed your babies. They'll probably have to be put on Weight Watchers when we get back."

Annabelle stood up and said, "Okay. We'll leave tomorrow morning at daybreak. I'll pick you up about 10:30." J.B. and

Annabelle agreed that very little interesting in life happened before late morning.

"Uh uh." J.B. shook her head emphatically. "We won't be taking that piece of shit old truck of yours. I'll drive my Beamer. I ain't showing up at FAMU and Florida State looking like a sharecropper. I hear there are some fine brothers hanging out at both those schools and I want them to know that J.B. Jones is a woman of quality." With that, J.B. maneuvered her butt into an outrageous sashay as she made for home and her perfect husband.

Road Trip through South Georgia

"I can't believe we've been on the road to Tallahassee for three days and we're still in South Georgia." J.B. gave Annabelle the evil eye as they pulled out of yet another flea market. "I never knew there were so many dipshit towns in this state. We've been to TyTy, Omega, Pavo, Attapulgus, and now, Climax." A pause. "I kinda like Climax. Let's go through it again. I could use a multiple orgasm about now." J.B.'s evil eye had turned into a lusty glint.

Annabelle ignored both of J.B.'s ocular manifestations. "I know it's taking a while, but I've got to be thorough. I don't want to miss any of the shops down here. You never know when you'll pick up an important tip."

J.B. had noticed that Annabelle had picked up a lot more in crap than in important tips. The trunk of the BMW was filled with rusty utensils and dirty (not to mention ugly) old doodads. She was confident that Annabelle's new buys would end up adorning one or another of the aberrations she called art and tried to sell at The Artful Dodger. J.B. was just glad it wasn't close to Christmas or her birthday.

J.B. continued. "And I'm wondering how important we really are to this investigation. I think Buster was just trying to get rid of you for a few days. How come he hasn't gotten in touch to find out what you've found out?" Even though Annabelle was too cheap for a cell phone and J.B. had accidentally left hers at home, the roadside motels they'd stayed in during their South Georgia sojourn, while lacking many amenities, had proudly included telephones in their room descriptions. However, Annabelle and Buster had been curiously incommunicado.

"I was supposed to call Buster and let him know where we are and what we've found out, but, since we haven't found out *anything*, I just decided to enjoy a few days without talking to him." Annabelle was correct in saying they hadn't learned anything important about the death of PhaPha Eberhart. Questions about vegetables as erotica brought blank stares in some venues and snickers in others, but no one seemed familiar with rutabaga raunch or sexual squash. Annabelle and J.B. had been graced with lots of dogs playing cards, and pink and blue kittens frolicking in lavender gardens, but nothing remotely resembling the monstrosity PhaPha had left at The Artful Dodger. One redneck even brought out a collection of what he called "Darky Art"— stereotypical pictures of Negroes spitting watermelon seeds and running from snakes, their eyes popping out of their heads. Apparently, he hadn't noticed J.B.'s Nubian beauty, or maybe he just didn't care. Annabelle had been ready to knock the cretin's eyes out of his obtuse skull, but J.B. just went into her Butterfly McQueen act and kept calling Annabelle "Miss Scarlet" as she dragged her out of the door. J.B. had found unusual ways to survive in the South.

Late afternoon on the third day of the road trip finally brought the dynamic duo to the Georgia-Florida line, with Tallahassee just over the horizon. Annabelle could see J.B. brightening up, with the thought of a city within reach. J.B. enjoyed urban surroundings much more than rural environments. She considered flora and fauna simply to be elements that needed to be sautéed, drizzled, and peppered before being consumed at high-priced restaurants. If it had not been for Annabelle, the Internet, and occasional trips to Atlanta, J.B. wouldn't have been able to endure life in River's End.

As they settled in at the Comfort Inn on the north side of Tallahassee, Annabelle resolutely dialed Buster's number. She was afraid he'd cut her travel money since all of her investigating had, to this point, come to naught.

When he came on the line, Buster started with, "Where the hell are you?"

"Tallahassee," answered Annabelle, innocently, and then added, just to be annoying, "Where the hell are you?"

"I'm right here where you called me, waiting to find out if I've wasted the taxpayer's money on Mo and Curly's adventures at playing detective, or is it Amos and Andy? Or, in your and Belinda's case, Curly and Andy. Get it? Bald and black." Buster had a good heart but he wasn't exactly enlightened. Giggling at his own cleverness (a high pitched giggle, not at all befitting an officer of the law), Buster didn't seem to be all that interested in hearing what Annabelle and J.B had uncovered, which just so happened to be nothing.

Actually, Annabelle was more curious about what had transpired in the investigation since she'd left River's End than she was interested in sharing the fact that Buster had just financed three days worth of antiquing.

J.B. listened for a while as Annabelle nodded into the receiver and said witty things like, "My ass!" and "No shit, Sherlock!" Buster was apparently recounting all that had been learned about the murder since Annabelle and J.B. had left home. It seemed that Buster was much more forthcoming now that Annabelle was out of range. Of course, he probably wasn't telling her anything that hadn't been printed in the paper.

J.B. finally decided to go ahead and take her shower instead of trying to decipher Annabelle's grimaces and eyebrow raisings. She didn't have time to wait—she had hair to wrap and face cream to apply. When she got out of the bathroom a while later, Annabelle was impatiently waiting for her, biting her cuticles while watching a cooking show.

Charlie and Stella

HEY CAT, WHERE'S MAM?

She's been gone for three days, you idiot.

I THINK I MISS HER BUT I LIKE MR. JEROME'S CAT FOOD BETTER.

His name is George and he's J.B.'s husband and that's not cat food. It's gourmet leftovers.

I MISS MAM. SHE MAKES MY TAIL WAG. MR. JEROME WON'T TAKE ME FOR A RIDE.

What is that smell? Do you have indigestion?

IS MR. JEROME BROWN?

Buster's News

What Buster had told Annabelle was this:

the back door of Food World had been jimmied open;

there were lots of fingerprints around the door, but, with the number of people who used that door, it was difficult to learn anything helpful;

PhaPha was known around Tallahassee as being a bit of a Jezebel, and everybody knew about her adventures;

PhaPha had not been sexually assaulted, nor had she had sex within the last few hours before she was murdered; and

PhaPha's husband was still the prime suspect but hadn't been arrested.

Annabelle had left the juiciest tidbit for last. She held that information over J.B.'s head for a few minutes, aiming for maximum dramatic effect.

J.B. finally got tired of waiting and acted like she was going to sleep. She got in bed and closed her eyes, pulling the covers over her head. Annabelle crossed over to J.B.'s bed and whispered at the place in the covers where she thought J.B.'s ear would be, "Guess where PhaPha's sister, Deirdre, lives?"

"In hell with me?" asked J.B., wearily.

"No! Alabama!" Annabelle almost chortled in her glee, raising her hands over her head in a poor imitation of the high school cheerleader she'd never been.

J.B. sat up, her head wrap all askew. "Alabama, as in the same Alabama on the greaser's truck tag?"

"The very same Alabama."

"That does seem a bit coincidental. What does Buster think about it?"

"Buster says Alabama is a big state, but then, don't forget Buster is a fool." Annabelle sat back on J.B.'s bed, wishing she had enough hair to wrap. "I just think there's gotta be a connection. I sure would like to look into it."

"Well, count me out. I ain't driving through the back roads of Alabama. I've seen enough of the Old South, what with Georgia and Florida. I think I've been lucky not to have been lynched."

"Well, don't worry. Buster is reeling us in. He says he's spent as much money on us as he's going to. He doesn't even want me to check the shops here in Tallahassee." Annabelle jumped over to her bed and settled under her covers, pulling her pajama bottoms off and throwing them on the floor.

"So, that means we head for home in the morning, right? I'm actually looking forward to seeing old George," J.B. said, drowsily.

"No, that means we check the shops in Tallahassee. Since when did I ever do anything Buster told me to?"

The Art Class

"You have until lunch time and that's it," said J.B. as the BMW pulled out of the motel parking lot the next morning. "I plan to be home in time for one of George's special martinis."

"That's all the time I need. There are just a couple of shops here in Tallahassee I really like." Annabelle had given up her ruse of trying to help Buster and was moving in for the kill on salvaged raw materials for her artistic genius.

J.B. continued, "Besides, I don't know how many more hubcaps I can fit in this car. I'm probably gonna be cuffed just for having this booty in my ride. Who's gonna believe you bought this stuff when you got a sister driving the getaway?" J.B. gave Annabelle a worried look as they drove into Tallahassee.

Annabelle directed J.B. to a junk-art store downtown. When they got inside, Annabelle immediately headed toward the worst looking stuff; plastic fish, dirty old dishes, and broken terracotta pots. J.B. tried to entertain herself first by making faces in a beveled mirror that needed to be re-silvered, and then by checking out the back room where it appeared a painting class was underway. She noticed still-life materials set up on a table in the middle of the room. Her trained detective eye caught a rutabaga in the mix. "Holy shit! Evidence!"

J.B. found Annabelle in the dusty catacombs, where she was checking out an old Brady Bunch lunchbox. Annabelle asked, "Can you believe how much these things go for these days? If I just hadn't painted up all of my kids' old lunch boxes to make them into purses, I could be rich."

"Put that thing down and come back here. I think I've found a clue." J.B. was fairly vibrating with enthusiasm, which immediately got Annabelle's attention.

"What is it?" Annabelle asked.

"A rutabaga," J.B. said proudly.

"A rutabaga," echoed Annabelle. "Is it in a compromising position?"

"No, but it could be. Come on!" J.B. led Annabelle back to the workroom. When they got there, they took in the still life table with its array of vegetables.

A very short, very fat, middle-aged woman with exceedingly black waist length hair and an orange muumuu turned to J.B. and Annabelle and asked, "Would you care to join our class? We're doing still lifes." Three female students, also middle-aged but more mainstream in appearance, nodded as if doing so gave credence to the splotches of paint that seemed to be proliferating on their canvases.

Ignoring J.B.'s contemptuous mumblings about artistic types, Annabelle said, "No, but could we bother you for a minute?" Thinking she would need some sort of official identification, she looked in her wallet. All she could find was her Food World Most Valuable Patron card. She figured that wouldn't hold much water out of River's End, so she just asked outright, "Have any of your students ever done a still life with vegetables that had a certain—uh—sexual air?"

Giving Annabelle a contemptuous look, the art teacher drew herself up to her full height of about four feet eleven, fanned her hair to cover her big ass, and said, "No, of course not. I'm an Impressionist, not a Fauvist. My students follow my lead." Annabelle couldn't believe nobody in the room was laughing out loud. How surreal.

Change of heart. "Wait a minute. Let me think. That could only be that trashy Phayla Franklin. She took my class one time, and everything she painted looked downright pornographic." The now-helpful teacher had decided to come clean, wiping her paint encrusted hands on her muumuu, adding to the dress's sunrise-sunset, thrown-up Egg McMuffin motif. She went on to describe PhaPha's style, even mentioning the erectness of her eggplant and the rigidity of her rutabaga. "I guess I shouldn't be calling her trash. I heard she was murdered." Warming to her subject, she added, "She was a busy thing, though. There were always rumors about her. I bet it was somebody's wife who killed her. I almost shot her myself. The whole time she was taking my class, she was coming on to my husband, Walter." Peering over her plump shoulder, she asked, incredulously, "You saw Walter up front, didn't you? Now, why would anybody be interested in Walter? I can't even get him to wear clean underwear."

Walter did look like an unlikely Romeo with his suspenders and brogans, but, then again, there was no accounting for taste.

Annabelle thought of the greaser who'd bought PhaPha's painting and figured him for a seldom underwear changer, too. She
headed back up front and paid for her broken dishes and bent silverware before Walter's roaming eye (and his wife's eagle one)
could land on her. Having seen and heard enough from white
people, J.B. had decided to wait in the car.

CHAPTER 7

Back Home

"PhaPha painted the painting?" asked Buster, acting like he cared.

Annabelle and J.B. had arrived back in River's End late in the afternoon. It took a while to extricate all manner of metal and plastic from J.B.'s trunk and to check on Stella and Charlie, so it was dark before Annabelle called her ex.

"Yep, it looks like it. You can thank me later for this important clue." Annabelle was lying in her bed with Stella on her feet and Charlie snoring and slobbering, his head in her lap. It seemed both had forgiven her for abandoning them. Apparently George had fed them something rich and rank while Annabelle was gone because Charlie had gas. She had to keep spraying room deodorizer just to continue inhabiting the same space.

"Annabelle, I'm not sure if it means much. We still think it was her husband. We're just trying to get enough evidence to arrest him," Buster said.

Annabelle suspected that the "we" in Buster's response had more to do with the Georgia Bureau of Investigation than it did with the River's End Police Department. It appeared that the State people had more or less taken over the case. Her bet was that Buster was relieved. This was very much out of his realm of expertise.

"Well, from what I heard from all the people I talked to"—all the people being one corpulent art instructor in Tallahassee—"he sure had a motive. Apparently PhaPha spent a lot of time doing good works that had everything to do with indiscriminate sex and nothing to do with the Junior League. But I just can't figure out her leaving that painting with me. And then there's the coincidence of the guy who bought it. Then both of them dead..." Annabelle tried to move her leg since her foot was going to sleep. Stella graced her with a baleful glance and a little claw action. Charlie turned over, taking up even more of the bed.

Buster responded, "It could've been some sort of kinky flirtation device. Maybe there was a message or a map hidden in the picture. I've read about people who get off on that kind of thing."

"That zucchini did appear to be pointing north," Annabelle asserted.

Buster didn't get the double entendre but, then again, Buster didn't get a lot. He continued, creating his theory as he went along, "Maybe PhaPha's husband suspected the bum and followed him. Maybe he caught them in the act out there in the woods and killed them both, leaving the greaser where he was and making some kind of symbolic statement by placing PhaPha in the deli case. Like saying it was just another way of getting porked."

"But PhaPha hadn't had sex," Annabelle felt the need to point out.

"Okay, caught them almost in the act."

"I don't know...that just doesn't seem like something a banker would do. You know how clean they are. Just think about the blood, the dirt, the honey-baked ham."

"You know, PhaPha seemed a little long in the tooth to be running around and meeting men in the woods. Wouldn't you have thought that she would've matured out of that by now?" This was actually coming from Buster?

"I don't know," Annabelle answered. "I think Boomers are gonna be doing stupid things well into their eighties. When we get to the Autumn Leaves Retirement Home, there's no telling the sexual shenanigans that'll be going on."

"You wanna go ahead and practice for when we get there?"

Annabelle hung up in a rather rude manner and went to sleep, glad to be in her own bed, sharing it with Charlie and Stella, and not Buster. She slept, dream-free, with no obscene veggie fairies dancing in her head.

Hubcap Martini Tables

"I don't doubt that PhaPha's husband did it. I just want to know how the painting fits in and where it is now," complained Annabelle as she and J.B. sat around the framing counter in The Artful Dodger the next morning. Their Diet Cokes were either half empty or half full depending on world view and hormone level.

"You're just going to have to let it go," said J.B. "Get on with your life, as pitiful as it is. You got a free road trip out of it. You need to move on."

"I don't want to move on. I'm impassioned by the drama, the mystery, the tackiness of it all," emoted Annabelle, sweeping her arm in what she hoped was a dramatic gesture.

J.B. took in all the junk that Annabelle had purchased on their buying trip. "It's pretty obvious you're impassioned by tackiness. What on earth are you going to do with this new amount of mess?"

"I'm thinking of creating hubcap martini tables to go with my hubcap chandeliers. I could sell them as a set or separately."

"Oh, those ought to go over big around here. Who do you know besides George that can even make a martini?"

"I was thinking of inviting George to be my first customer. He could buy a set for you for Christmas."

"Actually, I've been considering becoming Hindu or Buddhist or something so I won't be celebrating Christmas, and I don't think those people drink martinis either. But thanks a lot anyway." J.B. quailed at the thought of an Annabelle Original Martini Table with Matching Chandelier gracing her living space.

"You know, artists are seldom appreciated during their lifetimes. I just might have to cut off my ear."

"Yeah, and you'll probably figure out a way to decoupage it to my martini table. Now, that would make it one of a kind."

Annabelle and J.B. continued their discourse for a few more minutes, their jab and parry being a part of the rhythm of their friendship. No one took offense, as offense wasn't intended. It was simply their way of showing affection without being sappy. In spite of J.B.'s derogatory remarks about Annabelle's need to create, she actually admired her and would've liked to have had a little bit (a very little bit) of Annabelle in her. Annabelle felt the same way about J.B. One never knows what makes a friendship work.

"Back to the case," said Annabelle. "What can I do to find out about the painting? What about PhaPha's sister, Deirdre? I have a gut feeling she knows something, what with her living in Alabama and all."

"Do they have telephones in Alabama? You could call her," suggested J.B.

"What would I say? How about, 'Are you missing a really smelly boyfriend?' or 'Do you have an erotic cornucopic painting hanging over your fireplace?'" Annabelle was getting that weird right-brain look that she got when her creative juices were in overflow.

"What the hell does cornucopic mean? Is that some kind of new fetish?"

"No, it's just a new word. Very new, since I just made it up. It means having to do with a cornucopia. You know, horn of plenty. Plenty horny. Vegetables. Get it?" Annabelle giggled, and then snorted.

J.B. got up to leave, saying, "That's enough for me. Don't quit your day job for a place on the review board of the New English Dictionary." As she looked around The Artful Dodger, she added, "Come to think of it, what day job?"

Annabelle spent the rest of the day *at* her day job, framing prints and originals for clients, mostly bird dogs with bloody feathers in their mouths or needlepointed magnolia blossoms. She hated framing the work of others, but this was her bread and butter (actually, low-fat margarine). For some reason, the denizens of River's End just didn't seem to get her genius but, being a true artist, she didn't really care. She tugged at her ear, deciding to hold on to it a bit longer, at least until her hair grew out some.

A Call from Maddie

Early the next morning the phone rang. Annabelle, mostly asleep, answered. "Deirdre?" It seemed the previous night had *not* been dreamless. In fact, Annabelle had spent at least a part of it chasing Deirdre Eberhart through the woods off of I-75. Deirdre kept screaming something about cheerleader tryouts and cold cuts. Definitely Freudian.

"Mama? Is that you? Who's Deirdre?" It was Maddie, Annabelle's eldest child. Maddie lived in the Pacific Northwest in a ramshackle house in the middle of nowhere. She was a weaver who augmented her meager income by waiting tables at an even more ramshackle restaurant. She lived with her boyfriend, Sam, who was learning to be a blacksmith, creating andirons and other yuppie accoutrements since horseshoes were no longer big sellers. Maddie and Sam divided their spare time between selling their wares at craft fairs and doing God knows what at Widespread Panic concerts.

"Maddie, hi. You caught me in the middle of a weird dream. What are you doing up so early?" The time zones from east to west and the difference in their life styles made communication a haphazard event for Annabelle and Maddie.

"Actually, I haven't gone to bed yet. It's still yesterday." Maddie hesitated before continuing. "Mama, I wanted you to be the first to know that Sam and I are going to be parents."

Annabelle sat up, knocking Stella off the pillow. "What? How?" Stupid question. "Oh my God, please get married!" She didn't even want to think how they'd be able to rear a child with their lifestyle.

Maddie laughed in that deep guttural way that Annabelle so loved. "I don't think anything that ghastly will be necessary. We're having a puppy."

Annabelle expelled a sigh of relief; especially since three thousand miles was too far away to ever leave the dog with her. "What kind?"

"A Black Lab, of course. He looks a lot like Charlie, but I think he's going to be smarter. But then again, it would be genetically impossible for him to be much dumber," Maddie pointed out.

"And who do I have to blame for having this stupid dog dropping slobber and black hair all over my house?" Annabelle gave Charlie an apologetic look; his was one of adoration.

"That would be me, and you're welcome."

Maddie and Annabelle chatted for a while about what was going on in their lives. Maddie had talked to Bobby and Susan, Annabelle's other errant progeny, within the last few days. Bobby lived in California, selling cell phones to aspiring movie stars and cyber-freaks. Or was it techno-geeks? Annabelle couldn't remember. She had a hard time imagining Bobby, with his earth shoes and 1967 Volkswagen bus, doing business with the fast and the furious, not exactly his first choice of compatriots. Susan, Annabelle's youngest, lived all over, trying to make it big, singing in a Ska band, strands of her hair dyed pink one week and purple the next. Not a one of them had health insurance, which made Annabelle nervous. She'd raised them to be free spirits, but had somehow thought that their futures would include marriage and their career choices would offer 401K plans.

Annabelle worked the conversation toward the big news, which was PhaPha's murder. Although Maddie had never heard of PhaPha Eberhart, she was intrigued by the gory details. "No way! In River's End? If I weren't already a vegetarian, the thought of a body in the deli case would do it for me." Erotic use of vegetables as still life materials didn't seem to bother her.

"You sound like J.B. She's off cold cuts for life. By the way, your daddy hired me to go to Tallahassee to check out the art scene there. He needed an expert to figure out who painted the picture that PhaPha left with me." Annabelle said smugly.

"Daddy was probably just tired of you giving him advice." Maddie could always get to the crux of the matter.

"Well, that too. But I did get a bunch of new hubcaps. I'm planning on making them into martini tables." Since Annabelle and Maddie shared an artistic bent, she knew her daughter, unlike J.B., wouldn't make fun of her plan.

"How about woven cocktail napkins to go along with the table? I could work up a few of those. And, oh yeah, Sam can make napkin rings." Maddie and Annabelle talked on about ideas that would probably never come to fruition. But the planning stage was so much fun.

As she hung up the phone, Annabelle thought about how much she missed her kids. Maybe they could get together for Christmas. It was hard to rein them all in at the same time. Those years of having them under her feet seemed so long ago.

Oh well, it was time to get up. There were chandeliers to be made and murder cases to be solved.

CHAPTER 8

Deirdre

A few days later, Annabelle was trying to figure out the best way to attach legs to one of her hubcaps when a thunderous rumble emanated from her front yard. She thought for a moment that George had decided to mow her lawn in an effort to maintain the neighborhood's real estate value. Hoisting herself up off the floor, Annabelle went to the window and peered out. It was just as well that a luxury lawn wasn't high on her list of priorities because it appeared that a Hell's Angel was parking his Harley on her grass.

To Annabelle's artistic but myopic eye, her visitor was a study in black and white. Black jeans, vest and tattoo, white t-shirt, snowy buzz-cut hair and pale skin. He was small but strong looking, carrying himself like someone who spent his time at physical labor, definitely not a professor. Annabelle was fearful of what an altercation between Charlie and her caller would bring and was glad her ferocious behemoth was closed up in the back of the house.

As he walked through the front door of The Artful Dodger, the bad-ass said, in a surprisingly feminine voice, "Annabelle McGee? I'm Deirdre Eberhart." On closer look, Annabelle realized that it *was* Deirdre, and she had *not* had a sex change operation, nor was she particularly manly—just strong and stark and uncompromised—a buffed up Emmylou Harris with a flat top.

For some reason, the flat top looked good on Deirdre. This was not the twit that Annabelle remembered.

"Actually, I'm now Deirdre Black. I removed my name from the Eberhart Family Bible a long time ago. And since I was always considered the black sheep anyway, I thought the name 'Black' would be appropriate." As she looked around the shop, Deirdre graced Annabelle with a beautiful smile, the only vestige of the old Deirdre that she could find in this extraordinary creature.

"Well, Deirdre, I would say that you've changed more than your name. You look great! Are you a Hell's Angel or something?"

"Not ever an Angel but close. Used to be pretty bad. Now I'm a preacher. I do prison outreach and I also work with runaways." An afterthought: "I also own a bike shop and repair motorcycles."

So much for Annabelle's theory about Deirdre being involved in the murder. The woman standing before her looked like she could've taken on PhaPha and her smelly beau, but Annabelle figured there had to be some clergy rule against strangling people and laying them to rest in a deli case. She couldn't wait to find J.B.

"So what brings you to River's End?"

"Your ex. He asked me to come in to talk about what I know about Phayla, which isn't much. We didn't exactly have much in common. By the way, Buster isn't a bad guy for a cop."

"Yeah, he isn't a bad ex-husband either, as long as he stays on his side of town." Annabelle's curiosity was getting the best of her. "Did you ever marry, Deirdre?

"Yep. I said 'I do' and signed 'I don't' several times. None of the marriages took but I got a great kid out of one of them." Deirdre went on, talking about her son, who was a pre-med major at the University of Alabama. Annabelle was often dumfounded at the undereducated and unconventional people who had offspring who did well scholastically and professionally. She, herself, had endured years of teaching, in part to instill educational aspirations in her children, only to have all three eschew formal schooling as an affront to their individuality and collective creativity.

Back to the matter at hand. "I'm sure you were helpful to Buster. Everybody thinks that her husband did it. It appears that she wasn't faithful."

"Yeah, Phayla had a penchant for picking up the wrong kind of men, including her husband. The type she typically chose would fill an abnormal psych book, especially when she was looking for recreation. The nastier the better. Our childhood was so screwed up, I was lucky to escape, even if it was on the back of a Harley."

"So, what brought you to The Artful Dodger?" As interesting as Deirdre's story was, Annabelle couldn't figure out the reason for her visit.

"Buster sent me to see your chandeliers, which, by the way, are gorgeous. My friends and I like hubcaps. I think I could probably sell some of them for you at our next bike show."

Annabelle had found her niche.

Charlie and Stella

HEY CAT. DID YOU SEE THAT MAN? HIS MOTORCY-CLE MAKES ME BARK. I COULD CHEW HIM UP IF MAM WOULD LET ME OUT.

Why are you under the bed?

Billy Franklin

"Annabelle McGee, Chandelier Maker to the Biker Set," J.B. hadn't stopped laughing since Annabelle had told her the news. "The Lord does, indeed, work in mysterious ways."

"Speaking of the Lord, are you donating anything for the Methodist yard sale on Saturday?" Annabelle was busy packing up her contributions.

J.B. gave a little shudder, imagining what was in those boxes. Annabelle seemed to think of the annual sale more as her personal one-woman show than an attempt to raise money for good works. Last year, she'd contributed wind chimes she'd made from canning jar lids. J.B. felt certain none had sold unless some thrifty Methodist had taken them apart and used the lids to top off homemade Muscadine jelly.

"Yeah, I've got some old clothes and purses I don't need anymore. I thought I'd take them over."

"Can I look at them first to see if there's anything I can use?" Annabelle perked up at the thought.

"That's not very Christian." J.B. pointed out, rather uncharitably.

"Cast not the first stone, Ms. Episcopalian. I'm as needy as anybody, plus I'll add that Annabelle creative touch and make it into wearable art. Consider it your cultural contribution."

"Then you'll sell it to Deirdre Black and the Hell's Angels at a markup and give the money to the church, right?"

"No, I'll wear it."

Just then, the phone rang. J.B. answered because Annabelle's head was stuck in a box, looking at God knows what.

"The Artful Dodger, where nightmares become reality. How can I help you? Oh hi, Buster. No, I'm just helping out while Annabelle figures out what she's going to foist off on the poor Methodists." J.B. batted her eyes and mouthed kissy face before handing the phone to Annabelle.

"Annabelle, I thought I'd give you a courtesy call to inform you to expect the bereaved husband at your door. He just left here, and God, is he an ass." Buster sounded pretty put out.

"You mean Billy Franklin? From what I remember, he always was an ass. What's he doing here? I thought he'd been arrested." Annabelle's focus moved from the boxes she was packing to the thought of Billy Franklin showing up at her door. She'd never known Billy well since his rich parents had limited his association with the unwashed masses of River's End by sending him from one prep school to another before buying him a degree at some college up north that nobody had ever heard of. It couldn't have been much of a college, since it didn't even have a football team.

"Oh, he's got fancy lawyers and a pretty good alibi. The best we could do was to talk him into coming up here for questioning. By the time we finished, I was ready to confess that I'd killed the woman just to get him out of my office. What a condescending jerk."

Just then the jerk entered the store, letting the door bang shut behind him. He looked around as if something smelled bad (other than Charlie). Charlie whined and slunk to the corner, his eyes rolling like marbles in a sidewalk game.

Annabelle quickly hung up the phone, trying to make eye contact with J.B. Before she could get a meaningful glance across the room, Billy Franklin, looking like dry-clean only in a low-end laundromat, walked up to the framing counter and said, "Well, I can see that Phayla's proclivity for hanging out in unsavory places sunk to a new low there at the end."

Annabelle wanted more than anything to point out to the rich Yankee-educated banker that the past tense of "sink" was not "sunk" but she figured that would just further alienate the bastard standing before her.

"And what can I do for you?" Annabelle was relatively sure he wasn't there for a chandelier.

"You can tell me why my wife chose, on that particular day, to visit this lovely little establishment of yours." Billy had that kind of syrupy, dissipated Southern voice that sounded derisive even in the best of circumstances. Although he had to be in his mid-fifties, he still looked pretty good, what with his manicure and his blow dried, silver-toned do. Billy Franklin was the type of man that Annabelle disliked most, the type who thought his blue blood kept his shit from stinking. She figured him for a mama's boy and wondered about his underwear.

Annabelle could tell that J.B. was enjoying the drama and hoping for a fight. Annabelle, on the other hand, just wanted to get Billy out of her store before she mentioned something about his daddy's kaolin processing plant polluting most of southwest Georgia. No wonder Billy had moved to Tallahassee. His penis was probably already small enough. He didn't want to take any chances having the end of it fall off.

"Well, Billy. Are you really still called Billy? Your wife came in here to give me a painting to sell on consignment. But I imagine you already know that from talking to the police." Annabelle didn't want to get into a long conversation with this man.

"Now why would she sell anything to someone like you? There are some good galleries in Tallahassee. She wouldn't need to stoop this low." He stopped and scoped out J.B., who was trying to keep a straight face. "And by the way, why is your girl over there in the corner smirking? Doesn't she have some floors to scrub or toilets to clean?"

J.B. got her fight all right but it was she, not Annabelle, who did the ass kicking. Words emanated from J.B.'s mouth that Annabelle didn't even know she knew, and she came up with a few really innovative gestures. It was only when Billy Franklin was high-tailing it out of the door that Annabelle had the chance to get in a few words about his daddy and the size and firmness of his pecker.

The Letter

Later that afternoon, Annabelle walked out to her mailbox, looking for her electric bill. Spring in South Georgia, that gorgeous azalea-laden interval between the need for heat or air conditioning, was usually a good time for low-usage fees and she was hoping for the best. To Annabelle, electric bills were like taxes. What she inevitably had to pay was based, not on economics or even weather, but on voodoo. Using her crossed fingers as a totem, she opened her mailbox and did, indeed, find her bill—a good one. What a great omen! She could now afford to use the Krispy Chik coupon that was also part of her mail booty. A spicy breast and tater logs sounded like a wholesome dinner. She would, however, need to eat in instead of carrying out since she was hungry and Charlie and Stella loved Krispy Chik as much as she did.

Walking back to her house and rejoicing in her good karma aura, Annabelle noticed a letter addressed by hand and post-marked from Alabama. Never letting discretion get in the way of curiosity, she cast aside all thoughts of Anthrax and opened the envelope. Maybe it was an order for hubcap chandeliers from the Montgomery Chapter of the Hell's Angels.

Instead, she found a note inside that said, "Quit nosying into other peoples business. P.S. I like your haircut."

So much for good karma.

The haircut that somebody in Alabama liked so much was standing up on end. Annabelle was shaking as she dialed the phone. It was probably significant that the first person she called was not Buster, her ex-husband, the Chief of Police, but J.B., her friend.

"Don't touch it. You'll mess up the fingerprints!" J.B. hollered into the phone. "I'll be right over."

Thinking that it might be a little late for the "don't touch it" advice, Annabelle did, however, drop the letter on her bed. Charlie promptly jumped up and sat on it.

A bit later, after J.B. had called Buster, Annabelle was sitting in the River's End police station having her fingerprints taken by the ever-officious Martha Mason. Martha had just recently added fingerprinting to her expanding repertoire of duties and responsi-bilities in the department.

"I swear, Annabelle, I'd be so scared if I got a letter like that," Martha emoted, her sausage-shaped curls standing at attention as she wiped off Annabelle's hands. "But maybe we can get some important clues when we check out the other prints besides yours."

Just then, Buster knocked and entered the River's End's version of a forensics lab, which also happened to be the ladies' restroom. Since Martha was the only lady usually in residence, dual purpose didn't seem like such a bad idea. The only problems arose when Martha had to go during an important forensics procedure. The good news was that, while Martha had to go quite often, important forensics procedures were few and far between in River's End, Georgia.

Buster said, "The fingerprints may be difficult to identify, but we're pretty sure the paw prints are Charlie's." Annabelle was glad that she hadn't eaten at Krispy Chik before she opened the letter. She didn't want to have to explain grease stains, too. She hoped Buster would let her go before the restaurant closed. If she was going to be murdered, she wanted to die with a stomach full of spicy breast and tater logs.

Charlie and Stella

HEY CAT, MAM SMELLS LIKE CHICKEN. WONDER WHERE THE BONES ARE?

Did you say chicken, Charles? I'm very fond of chicken. I think I'll rub up against Annabelle's legs and purr. That usually works.

CHAPTER 9

Blanche

Annabelle had inherited her childhood home and a small
monthly stipend when her father died. Frank McGee had
been the Postmaster of River's End for almost 40 years when he
succumbed to cancer. Frank had been an intuitive man, especially for a postal worker, and he'd known several things. First, he'd
known that Annabelle needed to leave Buster. Two fine people
apart, Buster and Annabelle were a disaster together, more so
after their children, their adored buffering system, began leaving
the nest. Frank had also known that Annabelle, with her artistic
temperament and lack of business acumen, would need some sort
of financial security. Lastly, and perhaps of most importance,
he'd known that Blanche, Annabelle's mother, would take off for
greener golf courses before his casket was fully shoveled over at
Whispering Pines Cemetery.

Frank had met and fallen in love with Blanche Wozniak at the
Woolworth's dime store where she worked in Pittsburgh just after
World War II and, against his better judgment, had married her
and brought her back to Georgia. Blanche, an unapologetic
Yankee and a veritable fish out of whatever river water was left
at River's End, survived southwest Georgia by playing bridge
every weekday afternoon and golf at the local nine-hole course
every Saturday and Sunday, all the while spouting her liberal,
semi-Communist rhetoric. This dichotomy never seemed to bother Blanche or her various golf and bridge partners as she some-

how counterbalanced her position on human rights with her memberships at the all-white venues that were de rigueur in South Georgia at the time. In spite of her busy schedule and socialist principles, Blanche wasn't a bad wife or mother, although she'd told Frank, in no uncertain terms, after the birth of Annabelle, that there'd be no others. Annabelle had never known what her parents used for birth control, hoping that it wasn't abstinence. She and Buster seemed to get pregnant just by passing the ketchup.

Blanche had proved true to Frank's prophesy and had married an old high school sweetheart within a year after his death. Her new husband, Arthur, had made a killing up North in industrial floor wax (probably using non-union labor) and was currently keeping Blanche in bridge mix and golf shoes in South Florida, which was at least a million miles and light years away from South Georgia.

Blanche's only convert to her liberal point of view during all of her years living in River's End had been her daughter, Annabelle, although she'd never made her into much of a golfer. Blanche had, however, certainly encouraged her daughter's creative pursuits. Being an only child, Annabelle had spent hours alone in her room creating glue-laden masterpieces that Blanche never failed to showcase somewhere in her house. The only difference these days was that Annabelle spent hours alone in what was now *her* house creating hubcap-laden masterpieces that would, hopefully, be showcased at biker conventions. For this, she had Blanche, at least partially, to blame and thank.

Buster thought Annabelle should go to her mother's in Florida until all of this mess blew over. Annabelle would sooner die in her bed with Krispy Chik in her belly. For one thing, Blanche was allergic to animals. Well, not all animals, just Annabelle's animals. Blanche had a miniature poodle named Karl (the name, not the breed, being the only remaining vestige of her leftist leanings) who, although he was a boy dog, put up with Blanche painting his toenails pink. Talk about lack of self-esteem. What was he thinking? Anyway, Karl didn't like either

Charlie or Stella. Blanche said they made him nervous, which, in turn, served to make *him* urinate yellow all over Blanche's white-on-white plush carpet.

And then there was Arthur, who had a gastric reflux problem. He was always belching and hacking. Annabelle couldn't believe the high price that Blanche paid for her greens fees. She would rather re-make J.B.'s old jackets into purses and give herself free haircuts for the rest of her life than put up with some old man with opinions and indigestion.

"I'll come over and feed the animals," Buster insisted, knowing of his ex-mother-in-law's aversion to Annabelle's pets.

"I can't go anywhere right now. I'm doing some work on commission for Deirdre Black," Annabelle argued. This was a lie but she was hopeful.

"Annabelle, has it occurred to you that the only person who lives in Alabama and knows about your haircut is Deirdre Black?"

Charlie and Stella

WHAT, CAT?

Did you hear that Annabelle might take us to her mother's house?

WHO'S HER MOTHER? THE BROWN LADY?

No, Charles, the woman with the squeaky poodle.

YOU MEAN THE CURLY RAT WITH THE BOW ON HIS HEAD?

That would be the one. I think that we both need to act sick and lethargic.

CAN I STILL EAT?

The Methodist Yard Sale

The Methodists had done a good job with this year's yard sale. Not only were they selling every pair of kneeless jeans and every piece of over-microwaved Tupperware within the town limits, they'd also set up booths serving all manner of culinary delights from Brunswick Stew to fried pies. J.B. and Annabelle meandered through the bargains, perusing the merchandise. Annabelle was considering a new artistic enterprise: creating throw pillows out of old sweaters and flannel shirts, and the tables set up in the church yard held a glut of stripes and plaid at extremely low prices. She figured that, if she started now, she could be ready to contribute a couple of her designs to the Baptists' November Bazaar, thereby acquiring cheap advertisement in time for the Christmas rush. Annabelle was singularly nonsectarian when it came to her blatant attempts to push her wares off on all races and creeds. Today, she was feeling particularly confident because her contributions to this affair were selling quite well, thank you very much. She'd seen quite a few Methodists and a couple of Presbyterians sporting her jewelry made from wing nuts and washers, and other objects typically used for fixing toilets and building swing sets. She made sure that she handed out business cards to all who seemed interested (or confused).

"Isn't there something in the Bible about God getting pissed at people who conduct personal business in the church parking lot?" J.B. asked as she ate a funnel cake. Annabelle ignored the comment, feeling sure she was doing the work of the Lord by enhancing the lives of the people of River's End, not to mention improving the home decor of some Hell's Angels over in Alabama.

A while later, as Annabelle and J.B. finished off a couple of foot long hot dogs, Annabelle's acquisitions sitting by her feet in plastic bags contributed by Food World, the talk turned to the letter Annabelle had received the day before.

"Buster thinks it might be Deirdre," said Annabelle, "since she's the only person in Alabama who knows about my haircut. But that letter just didn't sound like Deirdre."

"You know this how? Because of one fifteen-minute conversation with this woman?" asked J.B.

"J.B., she's a preacher now."

"Oh yeah, we know that all preachers are good, don't we? I can think of a couple of televangelists and about a million Catholic priests who probably won't make it to the pearly gates."

"I don't mean that. It was more how she carried herself and the way she spoke. She would never say something like 'nosying' and I feel sure she knows where to put an apostrophe." Annabelle got up to throw her napkin away and then sat back down, feeling the late afternoon sun on her face. It had been a gorgeous day, one that made her doubt there was someone out there who wished her harm. Walking home with her best friend, J.B., Annabelle decided, once and for all, not to worry about the letter and to continue doing what she did best: making her way in the world by coloring it from her own unique palate and turning sow's ears into her particular version of silk purses.

As they parted at the sidewalk in front of their houses, J.B. offered a final thought. "Annabelle, make sure you aren't letting your excitement about selling your chandeliers to Deirdre's biker buddies keep you from making good decisions about your personal safety. Maybe she's just using her interest in your work as a ploy to keep in touch so she knows what you're doing."

Before Annabelle could answer, Martha Mason rode by on her bike, hair inert and wing nuts dangling. "Annabelle, I like the earrings you made. I think they're perfect for my personality."

Annabelle decided to re-think her jewelry designs.

Donnie Bingham

Annabelle was on her way to Food World, which has re-opened. The store manager had gotten rid of the old deli case and had purchased a new, improved one, hoping that no one would remember what had last been laid out in the meat department. Annabelle was resolute in her desire to get past the squeamish feeling she had whenever she thought of Boston butt or honey-baked ham. Besides, both Charlie and Stella seemed to be under the weather and she thought maybe she could talk Donnie Bingham, Food World's butcher extraordinaire, into giving her some scraps.

Annabelle had grown up with poor Donnie, although he was a few years younger. Donnie had been one of those kids relegated to the classes in the back of the building, the "special classes", every year he ever attended school, from first grade until he finally dropped out at age 16. Donnie had always been a really sweet guy, but slow. He was so identified with his special education curriculum that when he was in high school he'd been bestowed with the unfortunate nickname of "Stringum Bingham" from the number of hours it was surmised that he'd strung beads, played with blocks, and cut out paper dolls, not to mention the many times he was strung up by the seat of his pants on the coat hooks outside of the principal's office. The best thing that had ever happened to Donnie was going to work at Food World, where, under the tutelage of old Mr. Johnston, he learned the butchering trade and became more important to many of the women in River's End than even their gynecologists and certainly their husbands. Most local hostesses wouldn't dream of planning a dinner party without first consulting the still cutting and stringing Donnie Bingham.

Annabelle had often wondered if Donnie's educational problems had more of a social origin than a cognitive one, since he seldom had the opportunity to interact with regular kids. As an ex-teacher, she knew that a great deal of research had been conducted in the education of "special" students since Donnie's time. She hoped that enough improvements had been made so that children like Donnie today wouldn't have to spend all of their school days hidden in the back of the building until they were finally old enough to drop out, but she wasn't sure. One of the things that had turned her off of teaching was the way certain children were treated in school, not only by other children but by some adults.

Although Donnie was well liked in the community, he was still considered rather strange and it seemed he had only one "real" friend, one who was probably just as odd as he. That friend was Martha Mason. Annabelle couldn't figure out why the two of them had never married but figured neither had the social skills necessary to pop the question.

"Hi, Annabelle." Donnie had lost weight in the last few weeks. He was probably off cold cuts just like everybody else. Annabelle figured that Donnie had known PhaPha, too, and wondered if her death had bothered him or if he even remembered her. It must have freaked him out that her interim resting place was his domain.

"I've got some good steaks for you today." It never registered with Donnie that Annabelle bought very little meat to begin with and, when she did, it was hamburger on sale. He tended to parrot the same phrases over and over. People were patient because of his genius with a carving knife.

Annabelle coquetted and fluttered her Maybellined eyelashes, trying to beguile poor old Donnie. "Donnie, my dear, what I need today are some of your best free scraps. Both my dog and cat seem to be off their feed. I know you're just the man to help them get their appetites back." God, she was going to hell, flirting with poor Donnie to get free meat.

One of the best things about Donnie was that he considered finding the proper scraps for Annabelle's animals to be right up there with filleting the Mayor's mignon. "Be right back," he promised as feet, spattered and splayed, set off toward that inner sanctum, the cutting room, the butcher bowels, for no telling what entrails with which to entice Charlie and Stella.

While she was waiting, Annabelle couldn't help but wonder if, one day, Food World would name a sandwich for PhaPha and sell it in the deli take-out area. "PhaPha's Filet" or "Dead Deli Delite" or something like that.

Charlie and Stella

HEY CAT. I PLAYED SICK AS LONG AS I COULD. I JUST COULDN'T PLAY SICK WHEN MAM BROUGHT THAT GOOD FOOD HOME. I HOPE WE DON'T HAVE TO GO TO THAT CURLY RAT'S HOUSE.

This salmon underbelly is rather delectable. Don't worry, I think our hunger strike worked.

CHAPTER 10

Heading to Birmingham

Annabelle checked her map, looking for the best route to Birmingham. She felt a little guilty after deliberately lying to J.B. and Buster. She'd even stooped so low as to evade the truth with Charlie and Stella. J.B. and Buster thought Annabelle was heading to Atlanta to show her wares at the Lakewood Antique Market. Charlie and Stella were (loosely) operating under the assumption that Annabelle had gone to a Weiner Schnitzel Festival in Milwaukee, wherever that was, and that, when she returned, they would be blessed with doggie bags full of schnitzeled wieners, whatever they were. At least that's what Annabelle had told them as she was loading the truck with chandeliers while they sat forlornly at the screen door.

"Now, you be good," Annabelle commanded her pets, "And Uncle George will bring you sautéed goodies to eat while I'm gone."

Annabelle wasn't worried about Deirdre Black. She considered herself a pretty good judge of character, Buster not withstanding, and figured that anybody who liked her chandeliers couldn't possibly have bad enough taste to have anything to do with laying out a dead body in a deli case. Besides, she would be in Birmingham just overnight; only long enough to attend the biker rally Deirdre had invited her to, in an effort to prostitute herself to an entirely new audience. She *was* a little worried that Deirdre's buddies might not have the cash to buy her creations.

From what Annabelle knew about Hell's Angel types, they lived on cheap beer, LSD, and pork rinds. She even wondered where her future patrons would house any chandeliers they might purchase. Maybe in their doublewides or at some place called the Hog's Breath Saloon.

As Annabelle headed west, she visualized what her newfound celebrity would feel like. Maybe they would make her an honorary Hell's Angel. Would she have to get a tattoo? She hoped group sex was not required as part of the initiation. Even though she didn't want to become some biker's bitch at age fifty, she was excited that someone was showing an interest in her art and she'd be glad to get all those hubcaps out of her store.

Several hours and a biggie-sized spicy chicken combo later, Annabelle drove down Second Avenue in Birmingham, looking for Deirdre's bike shop. Deirdre had told her to look for the turquoise colored, cloud adorned building that housed her business, which turned out to be called "Highway to Heaven." Cute. No wonder Annabelle felt an affiliation with Deirdre. In spite of their bad-ass independence and feminist leanings, they both still had that female proclivity for bestowing precious names on everything. When Annabelle entered the shop, she found Deirdre lying under a Harley, trying to fix a doohickey.

"What you need in this place is a nice hubcap chandelier," Annabelle offered as an opening line.

Deirdre continued working but answered, "We'd just have shit hanging from it if I ever even got it up – old rags and somebody's underwear, probably. However, I think you might find some takers at tonight's rally. How many did you bring?"

"I brought eight but I can take orders for more." Annabelle had seen a salvage place near Deirdre's store and decided to stop by there on her way out of town to see what she could find. "Where's the rally going to be?" she asked, wondering if the location would be safe.

"Oh somewhere downtown. I can't remember. A friend of mine is going to pick us up and take us. No, wait a minute; you'll need to follow us so you can bring the chandeliers." Deirdre finally hopped up from the floor and wiped her hands on her jeans. "We've got about an hour to get ready. Come on. I'll show you my apartment upstairs and where you're going to stay."

Annabelle followed Deirdre up a flight of stairs that emanated from a yard full of old motorcycle parts and rusted metal things. As her hostess unlocked the door, she had her very first feeling of foreboding, not so much from a fear of murder and mayhem but more from the thought of grease-stained sheets and Jack Daniel's encrusted water glasses. As filthy as Annabelle herself was, she liked to have some control over the origin of the dirt.

When Deirdre entered her apartment, Annabelle held her breath, expecting the worst and wondering where the closest Day's Inn was. The entry was dark.

Charlie and Stella

HEY CAT. WHERE'S MAM? I'M HUNGRY AND NEED TO PEE.

Well, where she said she was going and where she is are two different things. I can always tell when Annabelle is lying by the way she enunciates.

DID SHE LEAVE ANY FOOD?

George is supposed to come over and let us out and feed us.

WHO'S GEORGE?

Married to the brown lady. Remember? Now, quit leaning on me. Your breath stinks.

I THOUGHT HIS NAME WAS MR. JEROME.

The Biker Rally

A small scream escaped from Annabelle's lips as Deirdre turned on the light. "Oh my God!"

The place was beautiful! Deirdre, with her Hell's Angel persona and grease monkey/jailhouse preacher vocation, had managed to pull off what Annabelle, for all of her artistic posturing, never could. Deirdre's apartment was a wonderfully appointed, immaculately-kept haven of earth tones and ambiance, a mini jewel in the midst of carburetors and drag pipes. Annabelle made a mental note, once again, to coerce her jumble of good ideas and best intentions into some kind of final product, to sweep up the dog hair and clean off the counter tops in order to create this type of serene domicile.

After Annabelle had been shown to the guest room, she began unpacking the outfit that she'd brought for the evening. She'd spent a good deal of time planning what she would wear, not wanting to stand out in a negative way. After much thought, she'd decided on Buster's old Rolling Stones Steel Wheels Tour vest over a t-shirt and a hippy skirt that she'd bought for five bucks in a used clothing store. She didn't want to make the Hell's Angels feel that she was being condescending, afraid that they might try to rough her up or, worse yet, refuse to purchase her chandeliers.

After pulling together her look, finger combing her hair, and adding some wing nut accoutrements, Annabelle joined Deirdre in the living room for a glass of wine. Never once thinking her hostess might try to poison her, Annabelle downed the wine while checking out Deirdre's attire. Apparently Deirdre dressed much the same for social occasions as she did for work and calls to police departments. Black on white or white on black. Either way, on Deirdre the combination was stunning.

Putting down her wine glass, Deirdre looked directly at Annabelle and said, "Annabelle, it seems you're very interested in Phayla's death. Were you two ever friends?" Was that a malevolent cast to her eye?

A cold, dead feeling went up Annabelle's spine and oozed out of the top of her crew cut. She too put down her glass, which happened to be empty, trying to remember what arsenic tasted like. Was it liquorish or almonds? Both seemed to linger on her tongue. How stupid of her not to have told anybody where she was going.

"No, we weren't friends, which made having her leave that painting with me really strange. I'm just interested and want to find out what happened."

"Annabelle, I've learned from my prison work that it's usually best to let the pros handle things like this. I wasn't close to my sister but I'd hate for this case to get all botched up. You probably need to let it alone." With that, Deirdre got up and walked over to Annabelle and did a strange thing. She reached out to the side of Annabelle's head, and, in a low, almost mesmerizing voice, said, "You have something in your hair." She caressed a strand of Annabelle's currently almost nonexistent red hair, perhaps lingering a bit too long. "Oh, it's your earring, all caught up." She gave a tug, possibly too forceful, straightening the errant ornament. "I really like your haircut, by the way. It looks a lot like mine."

Just then there was a knock at the door and Annabelle prepared to meet her maker. After a brief prayer asking for forgiveness for everything bad that she'd ever done (she didn't have time to enumerate), Annabelle opened her eyes expecting the Alabama version of Quasimodo. Instead, there stood a gorgeous brunette wearing an outfit that had to have cost more than Annabelle's truck. Although Annabelle knew nothing about haute couture, she was pretty sure that this was it. On a positive note, she felt pretty certain that she could take this chick, all 100 pounds of her.

"Annabelle, this is Genevieve. Genevieve, Annabelle."

"My God!" If Annabelle hadn't been so worried about staying alive, she would've laughed out loud just at the sheer number of syllables represented in the room. Annabelle, Deirdre, Genevieve. What were their parents thinking when they named their daughters? It took the poor kids their first decade just to learn to spell their monikers and then the rest of their lives to either live up to them or, even worse, to live them down.

"Annabelle is going to follow us because of her chandeliers," Deirdre explained as the three made their way down the stairs.

Annabelle couldn't figure Genevieve. She certainly didn't look like a biker chick. Could Genevieve and Deirdre be lesbian lovers? Was Deirdre coming on to Annabelle back up there in her apartment? Annabelle wasn't so worried about getting murdered any more, but she certainly was curious. Her curiosity grew even more as Deirdre and Genevieve, instead of hopping on a Harley as she had thought they would, enfolded themselves into a russet-colored Jaguar. "Drug money," she thought as she stalled, and then gunned her truck, trying to keep up.

Hours later, Annabelle was lying in her bed in Deirdre's guest room, enjoying the luxurious feeling of high thread and low dog hair count on her sheets. As she pondered the evening, she reflected on how wrong she'd been about this particular group of motorcycle enthusiasts. Aside from their shared affection for Harleys and other assorted iterations of "Hoggery", the people Annabelle had met at the rally looked more like members of the Republican National Committee than bad-ass bikers. (George and J.B. would've approved.) As it turned out, Genevieve was a financial consultant, who, apparently not being a lesbian, was married to a very nice vascular surgeon. Annabelle had also met a kindergarten teacher, a dry cleaner, a golf pro, and a probate judge. What on earth had happened to the bikers of Annabelle's youth? Obviously, they'd become educated, bald, and fiscally and socially responsible. In fact, the reason for this rally was to raise not hell but money for a local charity. Annabelle had been so moved by the air of munificence in the ballroom of the Birmingham Marriott that she had, at the last minute, donated one of her chandeliers for the auction.

Despite giving away part of her profit and being a tad outrageously dressed (who would have thought it), Annabelle felt the evening had, all in all, worked out well. She'd sold the rest of her chandeliers, even though she overheard several of her customers mention hanging her masterpieces in their five-car garages. As she dozed off, she thought, not of the probability that she'd be murdered in her sleep, but of what she could create next now that she was bored with hubcap chandeliers.

CHAPTER 11

The Bathtub

The next morning, Annabelle woke up early and encountered Deirdre taking muffins out of the oven. She declined the offer of breakfast, afraid not of poison but of the amount of bran her hostess had incorporated into the muffins, which appeared to weigh about three pounds each. Annabelle suspected that she wouldn't make it home before the bran started to work on her uninitiated gastrointestinal system and, furthermore, she'd been thinking about a McDonald's bacon biscuit since first light. As Annabelle loaded her truck, Deirdre locked up and left for the gym. As she waved goodbye and cycled away, Annabelle thought about Deirdre and decided that she'd look a lot better if she put on a couple of pounds.

Mid-day found Annabelle back in River's End, no worse for wear except for a touch of heartburn. She stopped at Food World to pick up forgiveness gifts for Charlie and Stella. As she headed to the meat department, she encountered Martha Mason talking to Donnie Bingham. They looked to be in deep conversation, which seemed somehow oxymoronic to Annabelle. She scuttled away, foregoing her plan to pick up something fresh from Donnie, instead grabbing pre-packaged wieners before she could be noticed and taken hostage by Martha and her mindless chatter. Stella and Charlie would never know the difference between Donnie's scraps and Annabelle's cop-out. After all, either choice would have that enticing Food World smell.

Busted

Pulling up in front of her house, Annabelle saw her best friend standing at her mailbox. J.B. appeared to be waiting for her.

"So, how was Atlanta?"

"Fine. It was fine."

"Did you eat at the Varsity?"

"Yeah."

"How was it?"

"Good. It was good."

"Annabelle, you are such a liar. I know when you aren't telling the truth by the way you enunciate. Besides, I heard somebody leave a message on your answering machine. Something about meeting you last night at the Birmingham Marriott."

"What were you doing listening to my answering machine?"

"I was over at your house feeding your poor babies, the ones you abandoned to go to Birmingham to get murdered."

After pausing for a second to wonder what J.B. knew about babies, either human or animal, Annabelle decided to come clean. "Okay, okay, I went to Birmingham and stayed with Deirdre. But look! I'm not dead and I sold all my chandeliers. Here, help me get this bathtub out of the back of the truck and I'll enlighten you."

J.B. gave Annabelle a look that said she wasn't about to pull a dirty old claw-footed bathtub out of anywhere in her current outfit and walked toward Annabelle's front door, using her own key in the lock. By the time Annabelle had gotten her suitcase and Charlie and Stella's hot dogs out of the truck, J.B. had already found a Diet Coke and was sitting at Annabelle's kitchen table, saying bad things to the poor babies about their mama.

"First of all, why on earth do you have an old bathtub in your truck? What could you possibly do with it?"

"I'll think of something. It was really cheap. I'm thinking of making it into a planter or a chaise lounge. Maybe a dog bed."

Annabelle leaned against her kitchen counter and rubbed Charlie with her foot, wondering what it would take to get him to sleep in an old bathtub instead of with her.

"Weren't there any hubcaps for sale in Alabama?"

"I'm kinda tired of hubcaps. I think I'll move on to something else."

"Well, you're going to have to tell that to the woman who left that message on your answering machine. She said something about three chandeliers for her billiard room."

"I wonder if I can talk her into a chaise or a dog bed." Annabelle hated to create on demand. Three more chandeliers. She wondered if she could stand it. Maybe she'd paint them purple and enhance them with faux fur.

"Okay, you promised enlightenment. Get started." J.B. sat back in a kitchen chair, making it creak and pop, hoping Annabelle's wood glue repair efforts would hold one more time.

"Well, for one thing, Deirdre's biker buddies aren't what we thought. Most of them are loaded."

"Yeah well, we knew they were into the Rebel Yell."

"No, I mean money. They're loaded with money."

"You've got to be kidding. How did they get it? Running arms for the Contras?"

"No, from straightening teeth and trading stocks. Things like that. I swear, that rally looked like a re-run of 'Lifestyles of the Rich and Famous'. And the ones who weren't rich were at least middle class, educated and, well, like us. Well, maybe more like you. Some were even black. I may have to re-think the entire state." Annabelle went on describing her unusual evening but postponed telling about the strange episode with Deirdre and the earring.

Finally ready to offer her piece de resistance now that both Diet Coke cans were empty, Annabelle said, "One weird thing did happen just before we left for the rally last night. I want to know what you think since you're so good at reading people." Hoping that was sufficient suck up to get J.B. off her back, Annabelle went on to tell about Deirdre trying either to scare or seduce her.

As she talked, she couldn't tell whether J.B.'s look of disbelief had more to do with the horrific thought of Annabelle being murdered in Alabama or with the doubt that Annabelle was attractive enough to snare a lesbian. It kind of pissed her off.

When she finished, J.B. just sat there for a minute, looking at her. Eventually she said, "Well, you might as well try women since you've never had much luck with men."

"Only if I could find one who would cook and clean. And I don't mean bran muffins and carburetors." Annabelle continued, "Speaking of men, how come you were feeding the animals? I thought that was always George's job when I'm gone."

"George is seldom home these days. Something about promotion. I think he's involved with another woman." J.B. wiggled her eyebrows like Groucho Marx, apparently to indicate she was kidding.

With that, Annabelle got up and started trying to figure out how to get the bathtub out of the back of her truck. J.B. went home before she could be talked into helping.

Charlie and Stella

HEY CAT. THESE SCHNITZEL THINGS ARE GOOD. I'M GLAD MAM WENT TO THE SCHNITZEL FESTIVAL.

They aren't schnitzels, you fool. You think I don't know an Oscar Mayer Wiener when I see one? At least Annabelle cut mine up for me.

THEY'RE STILL GOOD. CAN I HAVE THE REST OF YOURS?

Damn! I just batted a piece under the refrigerator. Maybe if I turn over on my back and stretch...

Yard Art

A few days later, Annabelle was in her front yard, happily soldering wire to a bowling ball. Nearby stood her new bathtub, which, it turned out, wouldn't go through her front (or any other) door. Never being one to pass up making lemonade out of a lemon, Annabelle had decided to create a yard art fountain from her latest acquisition. The bowling ball to which she was affixing wire was going to be a woman's head, which would sit atop gravel, which would fill the tub, along with water, giving the illusion of a woman taking a bath in repose in Annabelle's front yard. All of this would be hooked up to a pump that would contribute a gurgling sound and water movement. Ignoring the worry of what George and the Baptists would say, she was also considering the idea of adding two metal funnels to indicate breasts peeking out of the top of the gravel water. She just couldn't figure out the toes, but that would come.

The morning was beautiful. It would be hot later, but not yet. Annabelle had her windows open so she could hear her small stereo, the one she'd bought from Sears after her kids had left home, taking their more sophisticated sound systems with them. She was wearing Bobby's logo-enhanced t-shirt he'd used during his short tenure at the potato chip factory, Susan's old junior high P.E. shorts, and orange flip flops left over from when they were popular the first time. Her attire was a testimony to the fact that modern science had produced man-made materials that lasted longer than childhood. Her kids were gone but their hand-me-downs remained.

Coming from her CD player was the voice of Chris Isaak. What she liked best about Chris Isaak was his yodeling. She figured it took a man with good self-esteem to yodel. Plus he was really cute and had his own TV show.

Just when it was all coming together, the bowling ball, the gravel, and the yodel, a black Mercedes pulled up in front of The Artful Dodger. Thinking it was just a member of the Mafia,

Annabelle wasn't that worried, until Billy Franklin exited from the driver's seat.

"Well, well, white trash in her native habitat. All you need is a refrigerator on the porch."

The thing about that particular statement was that J.B. could've said the exact same thing and Annabelle would've laughed. But coming from Billy Franklin, the words ricocheted off of her brain like hail on the tin roof of the VFW. Thinking of lethal applications for the soldering iron she was holding, Annabelle said in a measured tone bordering on staccato, "You've got just thirty seconds to get off my property before I call the police."

As the words were exiting her mouth, seemingly of their own volition, Annabelle cast a close look at Billy for the first time. His eyes were bloodshot and he needed a shave and a blow dry. Was that the hint of a wrinkle in his starched shirt?

Noticing that one wrinkle caused Annabelle to make a grave tactical error, one so common to women. For the first time in her entire life, Annabelle McGee felt sorry for Billy Franklin. Big mistake.

As he turned to leave, Annabelle called, "Billy, come grab this bowling ball for me. I can't hold it and the wire and the soldering iron all at the same time." When she looked at him again, she saw the tears.

Before she knew it, Billy had fallen apart in Annabelle's front yard, grieving over the loss of his wife, raging over his inability to control his world any longer, and wondering who would hold him for the rest of his life.

And so, that's how it came to be that Annabelle McGee could be seen sitting on her front stoop on a warm spring morning, embracing Billy Franklin in the midst of an old claw-footed bath-tub, a bowling ball, and a half truck load of gravel, with Chris Isaak singing in the background:

"I've been thinking a lot about you.
I'm so lonely here without you.
Ple-e-e-ease (this was the yodel part) *don't leave me on my own."*

That should have been an omen.

Annabelle Tries to Explain

As soon as Annabelle got Billy calmed down enough to leave with a promise not to tell anybody about his lapse in decorum and, of more concern, his testosterone plunge, the phone rang. Turning off the stereo, she answered.

"What the hell is going on over there?" J.B. was hollering so loud Annabelle could have heard her without benefit of BellSouth. "I've been watching out of my window for the last hour and the longer I looked, the stranger it got." J.B. stopped to catch her breath, and then continued. "I was just about to call Buster. Then, all of a sudden, you were draped all over that idiot husband of that dead woman. I might've been able to tell what the two of you were saying if I could've heard over that cater-wauling coming out of your house." J.B. must have been finished because silence emanated from Annabelle's receiver.

"Come on over and I'll explain. That's if I figure it out myself before you get here."

A few minutes later, J.B. was disdainfully making her way through the odd assemblage adorning Annabelle's front lawn, refusing to even acknowledge that her neighbor was not only going to leave the bathtub where it was but that she was going to augment it in some profound way. She found Annabelle in the kitchen opening a beer.

"It's kind of early and you don't even like beer." J.B. noticed that Annabelle had a couple of gravel nuggets imbedded on the back of her freckled thighs and what looked like tears and snot on the front of her shirt. She felt pretty confident that the next few minutes were going to be great.

"I need something cold and Bobby left this the last time he was home. Plus, my nerves are frazzled. You want a Diet Coke?"

The two friends sat around the kitchen table as if the familiar surroundings, cluttered with cat food cans and past due bananas, could help them make sense of the day. Neither was ready to concede what was garnishing Annabelle's front yard so they steered clear of the out of doors, which would've been a more cheerful setting.

Annabelle described Billy's meltdown, ignoring her promise to keep it to herself. After all, what she told J.B. didn't count. She said that Billy talked about his love for PhaPha and how he knew she had problems. He had, according to him, tried repeatedly to get her help for sex addiction or whatever it was that made her need to seek relations with other men.

J.B. was having a difficult time understanding how Annabelle could go from threatening to have Billy arrested for trespassing to becoming his confidante and surrogate mother. She couldn't get Billy's comment about her being Annabelle's 'girl' out of her mind, and, frankly, wanted one more opportunity to castrate the bastard.

"Black women aren't as forgiving as white women," Annabelle offered as an explanation.

"That's because we've generally had a whole lot more *to* forgive." J.B. continued. "Annabelle, you act like you really like the guy. I can't believe it. He's such a condescending ass."

"It's not that I like him exactly. I just feel bad for him. He's so sad and lonely and screwed up."

"That's exactly why women end up engaged to people on death row or in prison themselves. That creep was probably the reason why PhaPha looked for love in all the wrong places. I'm warning you. Steer clear of Billy Franklin. He's trouble." Then another thought. "In fact, you better be careful people don't start thinking you killed PhaPha. Having you hanging all over Billy

Franklin in broad daylight on your front stoop sure looks like motive."

Before Annabelle could finish her snort of derision at J.B.'s speculation, Stella and Charlie passed through the kitchen, indicating that their morning naps were over and it was time for lunch. Taking their cue, J.B. got up to leave, telling Annabelle, "Enjoy your TV show."

"You know I don't watch TV. I think I'm going to have to take a nap after drinking that beer."

CHAPTER 12

The Heavy Breathers

After lunch, TV, and a nap, Annabelle was working inside because of the afternoon heat. Her bathtub would have to wait until she had a chance to go to Wal-Mart to buy a pump and the nuts and bolts she'd decided to use for toes sticking out of the gravel water. As she was thinking about whether to purchase nail polish or paint for the toe adornment, the phone rang.

"Hello." Heavy breathing.

"Hello?" More heavy breathing.

As Annabelle was getting ready to hang up, a slurred voice on the other end said, "I think you know who did it and you're not telling. Why won't you tell me who did it?"

"Billy? Where are you? Have you been drinking?"

"That bitch Deirdre thinks I did it. I think *she* did it. She always hated Phayla."

"Billy, do you need a ride somewhere? You shouldn't drive."

"I don't need advice from you. You're a bitch, too. You remind me of my mother, always bitching."

With that, Annabelle thanked God for J.B. and her keen insight, and hung up. She only hoped that Billy wouldn't kill anybody other than himself if he drove anywhere.

A few minutes later, as Annabelle was making her Wal-Mart shopping list, the phone rang. Even though she figured it was Billy, she couldn't stop herself from answering.

"Hello." Heavy breathing.

"Hello?" More heavy breathing.

Unnerved and about to hang up, she heard Deirdre's voice. "Annabelle? Sorry for the heavy breathing but I just hoisted a Harley. Has Billy Franklin been calling you?"

"Yeah, he just did and I hung up on him."

"He's in pretty bad shape...nutty. He keeps calling me, too. One time he'll accuse me of killing Phayla and then he turns it around and says I suspect him. If he keeps this up we're going to have to do something."

Wondering which, if either, of the scenarios of who killed PhaPha going through Billy's disturbed mind were true, and just what it was they were going to have to do, Annabelle said, "Well, he seems to be hanging out in River's End. He came by this morning."

"Maybe you ought to call Buster and let him know, just in case. Or maybe I'll call him." Deirdre was employing that same tone of voice she'd used just before the earring incident in her apartment over the bike shop. Bossy and in charge.

Annabelle felt prickly and premonition-prone. Was Deirdre genuinely concerned or was she just trying to get Billy to shut up about the idea that she did the dirty deed? Annabelle assured her that she would consider calling Buster. Who was Deirdre anyway to tell her when to call her ex-husband?

Just as Annabelle hung up, the phone rang. What now?

"Hello." Heavy breathing.

"Hello?" More heavy breathing.

"Damn it! I'm sick of this!"

"Annabelle, what's wrong with you? I was just out of breath from watering George's damned Azaleas. He must have five thousand of them and he's too busy doing God knows what these days to take care of them."

J.B. Thank God. Annabelle told about her other phone calls, and J.B. agreed with Deirdre that Buster needed to be told about Billy's harassment.

"Well, maybe I will tell him. Better me than Deirdre. By the way, why'd you call me?'

"Just to warn you that George did manage to come home for lunch today and he was asking questions about that mess in your front yard."

It was so difficult being a genius in River's End.

Woman in the Bathtub with the Blues

Annabelle spent the next day outside putting the finishing touches to her bathtub creation. She was pretty happy with it, feeling that it had a certain amount of insouciance and *je ne sais quoi*, and other French words, too. The wire hair looked tousled with curls emanating from the holes in the bowling ball, the face indicated an air of abandonment, and the nuts and bolts toenails and the funnel nipples were all painted a rosy hue. The final touches came from the wine glass that she'd hot glued to the rim of the tub and the pump that gave the whole piece the sound and movement of a sauna and the feel of performance art.

Late afternoon found Annabelle sitting in an old lawn chair with her own wine glass, admiring her handiwork as the sun was setting. Just then, Buster drove up.

Looking first at the woman in the tub and then at Annabelle, Buster deadpanned, "Got company?"

"My latest invention, my dear Watson. Her name is Eleanor." Even though Eleanor wasn't a French name, it seemed to fit.

"Well, I think Eleanor is a babe and much quieter than Belinda. However, she can't take a bath in your yard. There have been complaints."

"George?"

"You know George would never make trouble for you. No, it wasn't George, but he's about the only person who hasn't called. Poor Martha has been on the phone all afternoon. She tried to help, saying that she thought it was a birdbath."

"Well, it could be a birdbath. I've noticed some aerial surveillance, but then again, that could be carrier pigeons carrying the dirty news out into the county." Annabelle looked really sad.

"Hell, Eleanor hasn't even been here long enough for her skin to wrinkle. I guess it's good to give the River's End big mouths something to talk about besides PhaPha's murder. What if I removed the boobs?"

"She's got to go, boobs or no boobs. I'll give you a couple of days to dismantle her." Buster sat on the end of the lawn chair, almost upending it. "One more thing. Deirdre Black called and said that Billy Franklin has been visiting you. Why didn't you tell me?"

"Because I feel sorry for him. I think he's becoming unglued."

"All the more reason to let the authorities know. I can't believe we still don't have enough to arrest him. Maybe this harassment thing will help if you'll make a complaint. I'd love to make the collar on this case. The GBI has closed us out and isn't telling me anything. I'm coming off looking like an idiot."

"I don't think he did it and I'm not going to make a complaint. He hasn't scared me or anything yet. He's just acting like a typical man."

"Damn it, Annabelle. You're so freaking stubborn. It's always been impossible to control you. If I didn't know better, I'd think you were interested in him." Buster stood up so fast the lawn chair gave way, throwing her and tripping him. Annabelle, with tremendous grace and superb focus, managed to salvage her wine as they both ended up in a heap on the ground.

Looking at each other laid out on the lawn, Buster and Annabelle started laughing and couldn't stop. What would the neighbors think about this? The Chief of Police and the town's crazy artist-in-residence frolicking with each other in front of God and everybody. Of course, they'd been wondering that for years.

Charlie and Stella

HEY CAT. WHO'S THAT LADY TAKING A BATH IN THE FRONT YARD?

That's not a lady, that's a bowling ball. Annabelle needs to quit fooling around and come inside and feed us.

The Match-maker

When J.B. came to visit the next morning, she noticed a 'For Sale' sign attached to the big toe bolt of the woman in the bathtub. She felt sorry for Annabelle, figuring the town harridans had won and Buster had paid a call.

As she entered without knocking, J.B. encountered Annabelle cleaning paint brushes. She gave her friend a rare hug and said, "George offered to talk to the Art Department at the College. They like avant garde stuff. They might even take it off your hands for free."

"You've got to be kidding. I'm going to sell it. It's one of my best pieces. I've just got to find the right buyer, someone who appreciates real art."

Relieved that her friend was being her typical ornery, uncompromising self, and she could quit being sweet to her, J.B. changed the topic to that of Billy Franklin. "Did you tell Buster about Billy?"

"No, I didn't have to. That damned Deirdre did. I have to tell you, I don't like her as much as I first did. I don't trust her."

"I think you're just jealous because she seems to have taken a liking to old Buster. Plus, you're no longer interested in selling your chandeliers to her friends."

"What do you mean about her taking a liking to Buster?"

"Well, you told me she said he was a nice guy. And she sure seems to want to stay in touch with him. Plus they're both in law enforcement, sort of."

"She's not interested in Buster. She's a lesbian, remember? You said the same thing about her wanting to stay in touch with me. She just wants to know what's going on with PhaPha's case, either because she loved her sister or because she killed her." Annabelle went back to her brushes.

"Annabelle, there's one more thing I want to talk to you about." J.B. hesitated, as if to garner courage.

"What?" Annabelle didn't think that she could stand any more bad news.

"The other day George dragged me to Faculty Lunch and there was a new guy there, some visiting History professor."

Annabelle didn't like the way this was going.

"Anyway, I found out he's not married. And he's really not bad looking – for a History professor. He was pretty interesting to talk to. He's traveled all over the world."

"Then what the hell is he doing in River's End?" Annabelle was not going to get sucked into this. She was not.

"Some kind of Eminent Scholar thing. He won't be here forever so if it doesn't work out, you won't have to see him at Wal-Mart for the rest of your life."

"If what doesn't work out? Don't say what I think you're going to say. The last thing I need in my life is some neurotic academic who probably saves his toenail clippings in a jar."

"Just go out with him one time. I'm sure his toenails are fine. He seems lonely. Be your accepting white female self. Hell, you were all over Billy Franklin the other day in your own front yard just because his shirt was wrinkled."

"That's what all of this is about. You think by my going out with this...this history person, I won't get involved with Billy Franklin. I knew it had to be something. You've never been a matchmaker before."

"I don't think you're gonna get involved with Billy Franklin. At least not for long because he'll probably murder you pretty soon, slit your throat or something."

"I'm being careful. Don't worry."

"Just go out with this man one time and I'll shut up. I promise."

A few minutes later, J.B. was feeling pretty pleased with herself as Annabelle finally gave in and kicked her out of The Artful Dodger. She'd managed, with her great human relations skills (and expertise with blackmail methodology), to save her best friend from certain doom, giving her something to think about besides what was to become of Eleanor and Billy Franklin. Now all she had to do was broach the subject with the new history guy.

Eleanor's Destiny

Annabelle was trying to walk Charlie, but, as usual, it wasn't going well. Charlie just didn't understand the concept of a leash so he continually choked himself on the chain as he investigated the world outside of his yard. As they careened down the sidewalk, Annabelle still managed to take in the flora that spring had wrought. Azaleas, dogwood, and wisteria, along with peach, cherry, and Bradford Pear trees provided a fusion of color and scent that were close to intoxicating. It was just too bad that Annabelle and Charlie were making the trip at such breakneck speed, taking a peripatetic route around trash cans and under mailboxes, not really stopping to smell the flowers, which made Charlie sneeze anyway.

As they made their way back home, Annabelle noticed a truck idling in front of her house. For a second, she thought the smelly guy had come back; forgetting that he'd met his maker somewhere in the woods by Interstate 75. Then she considered the possibility that Billy Franklin had traded in his Mercedes sedan for a truck. Probably not. Finally, she wondered if the new history guy was scoping her out and that pissed her off.

As she walked up her walk, glad, once again, to have her trusty dog with her, a man got out of the truck and approached her.

Dressed in a sport coat and tie, the man's sophisticated looks belied her first impression based on his truck, which at close range was pretty nice. Maybe going out with the new history professor wasn't such a bad idea.

"I love your piece," the man emoted, apparently referring to Eleanor. "What an aura of sensuality and decadence it connotes. Insouciance, if you will." Annabelle would. "I'd be honored to purchase it and situate it in a prominent place if the price is right." So he wasn't the history professor. He was a customer. How did someone so enlightened end up in River's End? Should she invite him in? Too bad she was out of chandeliers.

"Oh, are you a collector or an agent? Would you place it in a gallery? Somewhere in Atlanta or New York?" It was so good to have someone with class and style to talk to. Annabelle considered the possibility of an on-going collaboration with this man, perhaps taking power lunches at Tavern on the Green, or at least at Houston's in Buckhead.

Looking proud as punch and just as erudite, the man expanded his chest and said, "Not exactly, ma'am. I own a bar over in Columbus, right near Ft. Benning. One of my strippers lives here in River's End and told me about it. The GIs would love this little lady. We can unhook that fountain thing and use her as a big ole ashtray."

So much for artistic integrity. "Three hundred bucks." An afterthought: "Plus tax."

"Sold! I'll send somebody for it tomorrow. We'll probably need a crane."

CHAPTER 13

Everett Pipp

Eleanor was just being lifted into a big truck when the phone rang. Annabelle picked up as she placed Eleanor's blood money in the drawer of her seldom-used cash register.

"Hello." Heavy breathing.

Déjà vu—all over again.

"J.B.?" More breathing.

"Deirdre?' More breathing.

"Damn it, Billy. That better not be you!" More breathing, raspy this time and punctuated with a sneeze.

Getting ready to hang up, Annabelle heard, "Ms. McGee? This is Everett Pipp. I'm new to the college and Ms. Jones said I should call. I'm sorry about the wheezing but my allergies are acting up. I've lived all over the world and I've never experienced pollen quite like you have here in this lovely little burg. My nasal passages are a coagulated mess." He sniffed a couple of times to illustrate his point.

God, this could not be happening. "Oh, hello Mr...er, Dr. Pipp. I was just walking out the door."

"Well, just give me a minute first. Would you be amenable to going out to dinner? Ms. Jones seems to think we have a lot in common. She was quite persuasive in describing your many attributes." Sniff, suction effect.

J.B. was going to be so dead. As soon as she got off the phone, Annabelle was going to walk over to J.B.'s house and smack her. She'd rather be brutally murdered by Billy Franklin any day than spend another second involved in this conversation.

The geek continued, unaware of Annabelle's plans for J.B., "Ms. Jones told me you're an artist. I just got back from a trip to Botswana and I must tell you that some of the native art I found there is rather remarkable. I have some pieces if you'd like to see them. In fact, I have artwork from all over the world."

Oh damn, enticement. Annabelle loved African-influenced art. What to do? What to do? Would she be able to stand this man long enough to see his collection? Was he just using that old "come up and see my etchings" ploy? However, if that was the case, she figured she could take him. A person with coagulated nasal passages couldn't be too hard to handle.

She quickly made up her mind. "Well yes, Everett. Is it all right to call you Everett? I'm Annabelle. I'd really enjoy seeing your art collection."

"Good. Do you have a favorite restaurant here in River's End?" Krispy Chik was probably not what he had in mind. "I apologize for staying here in town but if we go to Macon or Columbus, we might not have time to go to my house to look at my collection. I like to get to bed early." Was the reference to bedtime a gauche invitation to sexual activity or, worse yet, really true?

"What about the hotel?" Annabelle asked. The restaurant at the old hotel, the Grande Dame of River's End, wasn't much for good food but it was pretty and dark enough that maybe nobody would see Annabelle with this dweeb.

"Yes, the Camden is a good choice." Everett was polite enough not to say that it was the only choice. "I stayed there when I interviewed with the college and I found it quaint and quite historic. Would Saturday night be agreeable? About 6:30?"

Annabelle said, "That sounds good." This way Everett could be fed and asleep by nine at the latest and Annabelle could still catch some TV.

"Alrighty then. I shall pick you up at 6:30. I think I can find your house. Ms. Jones told me the address."

There was J.B. being helpful again. Annabelle couldn't decide if she was relieved or disappointed that Eleanor wouldn't be there to greet the professor when he showed up at her house on Saturday night.

J.B.'s Closet

As soon as she hung up the phone, Annabelle, with great indignation, made her way over to her former best friend's house. When J.B. opened her door, she suspected she might've screwed up but decided to feign ignorance.

"He's got clogged nasal passages and he has to go to bed by nine o'clock!" Annabelle wailed, clutching her paint-smeared breast.

"Who?"

"That geek you set me up with. You aren't a very good judge of white men. I swear, J.B., I may never forgive you for this."

"But you're going."

"Yes, I'm going, but just one time." Annabelle appeared more flustered than she had at any time during the entire PhaPha murder ordeal.

"If he's so bad, why are you going? I know you well enough to know you aren't doing it just for me." J.B. seemed to be in the midst of changing her printer cartridge, and it didn't appear to be going particularly well. She had black sooty-looking powder all over her hands.

"I'm going because he's got an art collection. Art is hard to come by in River's End, especially now that Eleanor is gone."

J.B. had known the art thing would be the only bait Annabelle would need, and had made sure that Everett knew to mention it. He'd certainly had no trouble waxing eloquent about his collection at the Faculty Lunch.

"Well, since you're going, what're you going to wear? When is the big date, anyway?" J.B. finally got around to washing off her hands as she and Annabelle went inside to the kitchen. The soot landed in George's immaculate sink, but J.B. didn't seem to notice.

"Saturday, and I'm not going to worry about what I wear. What do I care about what this guy thinks of me? I just want to see his stuff."

Feeling confident that Annabelle's reference to stuff didn't have anything to do with Everett Pipp's anatomy, J.B. continued to lead her friend through her kitchen and into her and George's bedroom.

"What're we doing in the inner sanctum? No, we're not going to your closet. J.B., this is too much. I can't take it." Annabelle looked like Stella did when she got stuck behind the refrigerator.

"Now calm down. There's no reason why you can't borrow something of mine. We're the same size, even though my figure is much more curvaceous." Giving a little wiggle, J.B. started pulling pieces out of a closet approximately the dimensions of the produce department in Food World, and just as colorful.

As J.B. held up one number, Annabelle said, "My God, J.B., that's a suit! I've never worn a suit in my life."

"It's never too late to change your image. Come on and try this." J.B. was holding a rhinestone-enhanced purple jumpsuit that Annabelle wouldn't be caught dead in. Furthermore, she'd never seen J.B. in it either.

"I think I'm gonna be sick. I'll get back to you, J.B., I promise." Annabelle fled from J.B.'s closet, her bedroom, and her house, vowing never to let herself get into that kind of situation again.

J.B. chuckled to herself as she went back to her computer. She was pretty sure Annabelle was no longer mad at her since she'd quite skillfully provided her friend with a whole new problem—how to keep from having to get herself up in one of J.B.'s designer outfits to go out with Everett Pipp.

The Date

It was Saturday night and Annabelle was ready. She'd resolutely refused J.B.'s entreaties to lend her one of her outfits and had chosen, instead, to don the old hippie skirt she'd worn to the biker rally. Her one concession to current style was a black cotton sweater set she'd actually purchased at a retail store. She'd had to stick it in the dryer to get the wrinkles out since her iron was out of commission because of a batik project gone awry.

Annabelle decided to forgo her usual evening cocktail because she wanted to keep her wits about her. No need to appear too friendly. She did hope that Everett wasn't a teetotaler since she didn't think she could survive the entire date cold sober.

Right on the button at 6:30, a car pulled up in front of The Artful Dodger. On the few dates Annabelle had endured since her divorce from Buster, she'd never known how or where to greet her gentlemen callers, since her front room was taken up with her studio and the rest of the house was such a mess. She usually just made sure she was ready on time, greeted them at the door, and made the excuse that her big dog didn't like strangers. Not a one had complained about not being asked inside. But, then again, none had come back for a second date anyway.

Looking out of the window, Annabelle noticed that Everett was driving an old car. It looked like a Peugeot. A Peugeot? She hadn't seen one of those in years. What was it about college professors that made them want to purchase ugly foreign cars and then hold on to them for an extremely long time? It couldn't be the money. Just keeping those old relics running had to cost more than buying a new one. Annabelle figured it for some kind of reverse snobbery.

Everett eased himself out of his car and made his way to the front door. From what Annabelle could tell through her less-than-clean window, he didn't look that bad. At least he wasn't wearing an ascot, which Annabelle had feared after their phone conversation. He was of average size and was balding. Next to men with ponytails, Annabelle liked bald men best, although she drew the line at bald men *with* ponytails. There was something about bald men's (extremely) high foreheads that bespoke (often wrongly) of high intelligence. In addition, Everett was conservatively dressed, which Annabelle also liked in a man. Just because she didn't dress particularly well didn't mean that her dates should-n't. Maybe she wouldn't kill J.B. after all.

Annabelle answered the door before Everett could ring the bell, which appeared to surprise him, and elicited a short cough-ing spell.

"Hi, Everett. I'm ready."

"Do you think that I could have a glass of water? This pollen is killing me." Everett did look to be in some distress. His pate was glistening as his hankie worked on his nose.

Oh God, what to do now? "Okay, but I need for you to stay here. I have a really big dog who doesn't like strangers."

"A big dog? I'm allergic to dogs, too."

"Good. Well, it's good that you're staying out here. I'll be right back with your water." Annabelle finally found a glass that wouldn't embarrass her too badly in the back of her cabinet and saved poor Everett's life with her ministrations.

After they got to the Camden, things calmed down and Annabelle began to enjoy herself. Although they were unable to have drinks *before* dinner in the veranda bar because of the pollen count, the two glasses of wine *with* dinner helped, and her date hadn't sneezed in quite a while.

The dining room of the Camden was decorated in a South Georgia version of Rococo. Corinthian pillars, ferns, and fusti-ness proliferated over the cracked marble floors, along with white cloth bedecked tables already set with big glasses for sweet tea, the drug of choice for most Southerners.

Everett turned out to be a minimally interesting conversa-tionalist, although he never once asked Annabelle anything about herself. He did know a lot about folk art, which was Annabelle's passion. And, in spite of the fact that the wait staff at the hotel restaurant was made up of college students who would've just as soon been hanging out with their friends down the block at the local beer joint, the food wasn't bad this time. Annabelle had the salmon and Everett the baked chicken (he was allergic to seafood).

Eventually it was time to leave and go to Everett's house to see his collection. Annabelle was excited about the prospect of experiencing some good examples of African and Asian art, but worried that her date might try to put the move on her. Even though his clogged passages should have rendered him uninterested in sex, she'd never known a man who wouldn't at least attempt to rise to the occasion, even if more in theory than in practice.

As the Peugeot pulled up in front of Everett's house, Annabelle was ready to try to weasel out, to take a rain check on the collection, even though she really wanted to see it. Just as she was trying to come up with some kind of plausible excuse, Everett turned to her, took her hand in his, and said proudly, "Mother is waiting up for us. She's the *real* art expert. She accompanies me on all of my trips." He looked cautiously optimistic and added, "I'm sure you'll like Mother a lot."

Annabelle bestowed a radiant smile on her date (the first one of the evening) and said, sincerely, "Everett, I will be so happy to meet your mother."

Billy Again

As they pulled up in front of Annabelle's house at nine sharp, it looked like Everett would have his beauty rest and Annabelle would get her TV fix. That was until she noticed the Mercedes parked next to the curb, just a few feet down from her house. It had Florida tags.

Deciding that Everett Pipp, what with his mucous-enhanced debilitation, might not be an apt pugilistic adversary to a drunken Billy Franklin, Annabelle told him not to bother to see her to the door. Everett looked relieved. It hadn't gone all that well with Mother. Although Mother was an absolute wellspring of information about the art that she and her devoted son had acquired in their extensive travels together, she seemed much more interested in checking out Annabelle from the top of her pixie cut to the hem of her hippie skirt and asking all the questions Everett had failed to ask during dinner. Mother didn't seem to like the answers.

Offering thanks and a goodnight, Annabelle unfolded herself from the Peugeot, slammed the door, and then watched it putter down the street, exhaust fumes from the antiquated engine mitigating the fragrance and mostly unpolluted air of the warm spring night. However, Annabelle didn't have time to worry about the ozone layer. She was furious at Billy and she was going to put a stop to his visits.

Walking up to the Mercedes, she beat on the window and screamed, "Billy Franklin, you get out of that car this minute. I want to talk to you!" She didn't care if he was drunk or dangerous or crazy or what, or who was watching though darkened windows, TVs turned low. Annabelle was so mad she felt impervious to physical danger or neighborhood gossip.

Like the little boy he still was, Billy obeyed and immediately got out of the car. He didn't look drunk or crazy, just tired. Dark circles underscored his sad eyes and his shirt had escaped from his pants.

"Don't be mad. I just didn't have anywhere to go. The bank put me on leave and I can't stand being at home. Can I stay with you? Just for a few days?"

"What?" Annabelle was incredulous. She crossed her arms and leaned back against the ebony-toned status icon that was Billy's car, knowing there was little chance of getting her sweater dirty. "How can you go from calling me a bitch like your mother to wanting to stay with me? Billy, I think you need some help. Some kind of professional help."

"I just need somebody warm. Not cold like Phayla." Billy looked into Annabelle's eyes. She couldn't tell if he was alluding to PhaPha alive or dead, laid out with the cold cuts. Either way, the comment was chilling and his look was veering back toward crazy.

"Well, my body isn't available for keeping anybody warm but me, so you'd better move on." Annabelle was ready to stalk off in moral indignation.

"I didn't mean it like that. Annabelle, I really like you. You're the only one I can talk to. Please let me come inside for just a minute. Just give me a cup of coffee."

First a glass of water, now a cup of coffee. Who did these people think she was, Martha Stewart?

"I'll bring you a cup of instant, but you have to stay outside. You can sit on the steps. I have a big dog that doesn't like strangers." Annabelle had forgotten that Billy had already been inside and had survived Charlie's best surveillance tactics. She continued, "Just stay here. I'll be right back and we can talk for a little while."

So that's how it came to be that Annabelle McGee could be seen sitting on her front stoop on a warm spring evening, consoling Billy Franklin without Eleanor to chaperone.

A while later, after he'd finished his diatribe about all the terrible things that had befallen him of late and how everybody knew who killed Phayla but him, Billy looked at Annabelle and asked, "What happened to your bathtub?"

The Morning After

"Okay, tell me all about your date." J.B. was over the next morning before Annabelle had a chance to unlock the door. Apparently she was the only neighbor who'd missed Annabelle's après-date date.

"Which one?" Annabelle looked tired and cranky, with the hair on one side of her head standing out like someone signaling a left-hand turn.

"What do you mean, which one? Everett, of course. What did you end up wearing? I hope it wasn't that long skirt left over from the '60s. That thing is skanky. My silk wrap dress would've been perfect, but no, you have to be your own individual no-style self. Did you like him? Did he like you?" J.B. was so into Annabelle's fantasy evening that she hadn't stopped to think about what her friend had asked. "Wait a minute. Did you mean 'Which date?' when you asked 'Which one'? Did you have more than one date?"

"Let me start with the first one. Everett seemed to like me okay and I could stand him. However, Mother was a different matter."

"Mother? Does he have a big dog named 'Mother'? That's a pretty bad name for a dog. Must be mean." J.B. had downed too much caffeine waiting for Annabelle to wake up and answer her questions.

"No, Everett has a mother named 'Mother', but she does make a pretty good watch dog. Mother doesn't appreciate any interference when it comes to her *very* close relationship with her son. I think she put the evil eye on me." Annabelle gave a little shudder and tried to flatten her hair.

"Yikes. He sure didn't mention Mother at the Faculty Lunch. I'm sorry, Annabelle." After a second, J.B. added, "But hey, at least it kept you away from Billy Franklin for an evening."

Annabelle shuddered again. "Wrong. Get ready for date number two."

J.B. looked horrified as Annabelle recounted Billy's visit the night before. "Annabelle, what on earth are you thinking? You rebuff a perfectly nice man just because he's got a devoted mother and you allow this...this murderer on your property at all hours of the night. Is it his shit-head, bad-boy persona or the fact that you would've never had a chance at him thirty years ago when you weren't a cheerleader like PhaPha?"

Ouch! That hurt, partly because it bordered on the truth. Was Annabelle going through some kind of delayed adolescence? She had to admit that, in a perverse way, she was attracted to Billy Franklin, the very type of man she disliked most. Maybe it was an oxford-cloth overdose or something. Maybe it was the Eau de

Canoe or something. Maybe she was the one who needed professional help or something.

Nonsense. She just felt sorry for him, so she retorted,
"Nonsense, I just feel sorry for him. I don't think he's dangerous
or guilty. I believe he really loved PhaPha."

J.B. wasn't to be dissuaded. "I think he loved her, too, which
was probably why he killed her. An act of passion. Remember
how Buster described the scene in the deli case? He said PhaPha
was laid out almost reverently. That sounds like someone who
loved her very much." She continued, "Bottom line is, you need
to stay away from Billy Franklin. Even in the best of circumstances, that man would only break your heart."

Annabelle did have some difficulty imagining Billy and her
in any kind of long-lasting relationship, even if he turned out not
to be a murderer. She had the feeling that he wouldn't take too
well to either hubcap chandeliers or yodeling, and felt pretty sure
that, once all of this was over, he would go back to being the
puffed up asshole that his bloodline preordained him to be. J.B.
was right. Billy Franklin would have to find another warm body
to see him through his hard times.

"Oh, Annabelle, one last question. You and Billy last night.
You didn't...you know." J.B. looked almost undone.

"J.B., are you asking if I went to bed with him?" Annabelle
asked. "Absolutely not. I'm not that stupid." A hesitation, and
then, "I couldn't have, even if I'd wanted to. Could you imagine
Billy Franklin and Charlie and Stella and me all in bed together?"

J.B. couldn't imagine that and felt better.

Charlie and Stella

HEY CAT. WHERE WAS MAM LAST NIGHT? I DON'T
LIKE IT WHEN SHE'S GONE. I LOVE MAM.

She forgot to change our water, too.

CHAPTER 14

Chinaberry Necklaces

Billy must have found his other warm body because Annabelle hadn't heard from him in over a week. She had to admit she was relieved, and hoped he'd been able to go back to Tallahassee, back to work, and back to what was left of his life. Besides, Annabelle was too busy to worry about Billy Franklin or PhaPha's murder.

On her date the other evening, she'd admired a piece of African jewelry made from some kind of dried berry in Everett Pipp's collection, and had taken it upon herself to try to recreate the style with the chinaberries that were so exasperatingly profuse in southwest Georgia. She felt that a natural materials line would be a nice addition to her collection of wing nut earrings. Although chinaberries were known to be messy and poisonous, their sheer abundance and free price made them perfect raw materials for Annabelle's art. She'd just have to be careful not to eat them and to admonish prospective jewelry buyers to do the same. Her plans were to string them, cook them, and then paint them if their color didn't turn out to be any more attractive after cooking than it was currently.

However, she was having a problem. Being a person who never took much of an interest in horticulture, Annabelle had failed to realize that optimal berry time was fall and not spring, and that the few berries that she'd been able to locate, so far, were left over from the previous autumn. However, so as not to be a quitter, she'd decided to give it one last try.

"Charlie, come on boy! You want to go for a ride? You want to go for a ride?" Charlie came charging out from under Annabelle's covers, looking appropriately wound up, wagging his tail and dodging the leash. "Okay, come on, baby. I'll put the leash on you later. You are such a good boy," she crooned with only partial insincerity. Aside from the leash, Annabelle was carrying a basket for the berries, and a cold Diet Coke.

Late the previous afternoon, Annabelle had noticed a big old chinaberry tree that seemed to have held on to its fruit adorning one of the main streets in River's End. Pulling up next to the tree, Annabelle reached for the basket, the leash, and the Diet Coke before opening the door of the truck. As she was attempting to make her exit, Charlie evidently decided she was taking too long and jumped over her, over the basket, over the leash, and almost over the Diet Coke, which spilled in Annabelle's lap. "Damn it, Charlie! Come back here, you shit!" She attempted to dab at the spill with the wadded up leash.

When she thought to look up, Charlie had taken off to wherever his nose was leading him, proceeding up and down sidewalks and through flowerbeds to the small houses that lined the street, places that seemed to Charlie to need a visit from a friendly dog. Knowing that catching him would be difficult under the circumstances, Annabelle set out with a determined stride. "Come back here, you fool!" She held out the leash as if there were a chance in hell it would entice him into coming to her.

One of the houses, one that was painted an unfortunate shade of ultramarine blue, seemed to be especially appealing to Charlie, who made several pilgrimages to its front porch and, finally, unbelievably, put his paws up on the window ledge and looked inside. This was getting embarrassing. Annabelle was going to have to catch him before they both got arrested.

Just as she raced up the sidewalk to the blue house, Charlie placed his weight on the front door, scratched a couple of times and, holy shit, it opened. Thinking a lawsuit was in order or even some pound and prison time, Annabelle rushed in to try to catch him and get him out before anybody knew they were there. As she charged into the small entry, expecting to encounter her bad dog and perhaps an irate homeowner, what she stumbled onto was something else entirely.

What Annabelle witnessed in that blue house on that spring day in River's End, Georgia, was the very same ugly painting of erotically-positioned vegetables PhaPha had left at The Artful Dodger, the same one the smelly guy had purchased one day later with his bogus bills, just before they were both murdered somewhere by somebody that nobody knew. What she was looking at was PhaPha's Atrocity, her last (and perhaps only) known work of art. There it was hanging in the living room of the very house Charlie had broken into.

Annabelle looked at Charlie, stopping to re-evaluate his intellect. He *was* managing to look both apologetic and proud as he sat there wagging his tail and slobbering on the shag carpet.

Whose house was this anyway?

Charlie

HEY CAT, I MEAN, MAM. I'M REALLY, REALLY SORRY ABOUT COMING INSIDE. I DIDN'T MEAN TO BUT THIS HOUSE SMELLS GOOD! IT SMELLS LIKE SCHNITZEL. THE PORCH SMELLS LIKE SCHNITZEL, THE WINDOW SMELLS LIKE SCHNITZEL, THE DOOR KNOB SMELLS LIKE SCHNITZEL. AND THAT PICTURE OVER THERE SMELLS LIKE SCHNITZEL. I THINK I'VE SEEN THAT PICTURE BEFORE.

The Shrine

Annabelle should've left the house, right then before anything else happened, while she was close enough to Charlie to snap the leash to his collar and drag him out. She should've done that, but she didn't.

Instead, Annabelle walked over and peered closely at PhaPha's painting just to make sure, please God, that there weren't two such eyesores out in the world. No, this was it. The same painting, the same frame, the same zucchini.

Feeling confident because of her shrewd identification of PhaPha's Atrocity, Annabelle made the decision to see if she could figure out just who in the heck owned the house in which she was trespassing. For some reason, she didn't feel guilty or even afraid. After all, she was just helping Buster and the Police Department gather evidence, and she had Charlie with her.

When the sterile, plastic-covered-everything living room gave no indication of either ownership or sense of style, Annabelle moved on. Charlie seemed intent on doing his own investigation as he headed toward the kitchen. Following him, she noticed a clean sink and a full refrigerator, but not much else, no bills, no dental reminders, no dry-cleaning receipts, nothing with a name. She made her way down the short hall to what appeared to be a bedroom. Charlie was right behind her.

Opening the door to a room that she had no business entering in a house that she had no business being in, Annabelle was greeted with a sight that made the experience of encountering PhaPha's Atrocity pale in comparison.

It was a bedroom, a normal-looking bedroom with the requisite furniture and accessories, a room not unlike millions of others, except that this normal-looking bedroom was set up as a shrine to Phayla Eberhart. Pictures were everywhere, pictures from high school, newspaper clippings and photos from her life as an adult, all enlarged or framed or placed in a montage that covered the walls. A veritable plethora of PhaPha-ness. As Annabelle gazed around the room in disbelief, she saw pictures of PhaPha's wedding (without Billy), Gala Committee photos, PhaPha with the cheerleading squad, and, mounted over the bed, the biggest and most prominent icon of all, a poster-sized enlargement of PhaPha on the Homecoming Court, wearing a bouffant hairdo and an ultramarine gown.

The absolute creepiness of it all made Annabelle shiver like Charlie after a bath. However, her curiosity was greater than the sum of her fears, so she stayed and snooped some more. In doing so, she noticed a pile of dirty socks, a black and white TV, a trash can full of empty Mountain Dew cans, and a stack of letters tied with a blue bow.

It was one thing to enter a person's home without permission, to check out his refrigerator, or even to violate the sanctity of his bedroom. But to look at his personal mail—especially mail that had been tied up in a blue ribbon—was just too much. To do so was going too far. Annabelle refused to stoop that low.

The letters were addressed to Donnie Bingham.

Trapped

"Just what the fuck is going on in here?" an angry voice demanded from somewhere behind Annabelle. She almost jumped out of her flip-flops, knowing that Donnie Bingham, the probable murderer of Phayla Eberhart, was home from his job at Food World. He had to be pissed not only because she was in his house reading his mail but also because Charlie was asleep and snoring on his bed.

Lacking any kind of plausible explanation, Annabelle still attempted to give it a try. As she turned to speak, ready to say something about Charlie thinking he'd smelled smoke, she saw, not Donnie Bingham looking unhinged, but Billy Franklin. And on the craze-o-meter, Billy was at full-tilt.

Annabelle stammered, "How? What?"

"I've been following you for days. I knew you knew who did it. It was just a matter of time and looking behind enough bushes." Billy must have spent hours doing surveillance behind chinaberry trees. "Now, this! What kind of screwed-up creep would do this?" He walked around the room, looking at the mementos of his late wife's life, and shaking his head in disbelief. "I'm going to kill the bastard. Who is he?"

"First of all, I didn't know anything. Believe it or not, Charlie brought me here."

"Who's Charlie?"

"My dog." They both looked at Charlie snoozing on the bed. Annabelle shrugged. She didn't get it either.

"As far as whose house this is, he's some guy we knew in high school. Donnie Bingham. He's a little slow. I can't imagine he'd have what it takes to kill somebody."

"He was obviously stalking my wife." Billy stopped as if to gain some control, and continued, "He had what it took to stalk my wife. I'm sure he could manage to strangle her, too, the pervert."

"Billy, wait! Look at these letters." Annabelle held out the ribbon-wrapped bundle. "Look who all these letters are from. They're from PhaPha. It looks like they had some kind of relationship." She was hoping Billy would make her open and read the letters but he didn't seem at all interested in what they had to say.

"All the more reason for the bastard to kill her. He knew he could never have her. She belonged to me." Billy's ironic assertion of ownership made Annabelle's stomach spasm.

Annabelle didn't think mentioning the notion that the smelly guy could've killed PhaPha would placate Billy or change his mind at this point. She was now more than ready to do what she should've done before he showed up. "Hey, why don't we call Buster now that we know about all this? Let's let him handle it."

"Screw that! I'm gonna handle this situation myself. I've got something in the car that can take care of this asshole."

As Billy ran out of the still wide-open front door of Donnie Bingham's ultramarine-colored house and headed to his Mercedes, which was parked behind her truck, Annabelle made for the kitchen to find a phone to call Buster. She figured Billy was looking for a gun, possibly the same gun that had killed PhaPha's less-than-delectable paramour in the woods by I-75.

Finding no phone in the kitchen, Annabelle rushed back to the bedroom. "Charlie, do you see a phone?" Charlie opened and closed one eye. Must have been a 'no'. It seemed that Donnie either didn't have a phone at all, or like so many others, had gone totally cellular. She was trapped in a blue house with no phone, with a crazy Billy Franklin, who would be coming back in just a minute with a gun, and it didn't look like Charlie was in his protective mode.

When Billy returned he was carrying not a gun as Annabelle had feared, but a nine iron, with which he did a practice swing in Donnie Bingham's living room, barely missing PhaPha's Atrocity.

Coming through the door right behind him was Deirdre Black.

CHAPTER 15

A Hostage Situation

Annabelle looked past Billy and asked, "What are *you* doing here?" She hadn't noticed Deirdre's Harley attaching itself to the growing succession of vehicles parked across from Donnie's house; first Annabelle's truck, then Billy's Mercedes, now a big old Hog.

When he heard Annabelle's question, Billy turned and almost hit Deirdre in the head with his golf club as he also asked, "What are *you* doing here?"

Deirdre looked at Billy and said, "I've been following you for days, since Annabelle told me you were hanging around River's End. I wanted to see what you were up to." She turned to Annabelle and asked, "Just what is your fixation with trees?"

Before Annabelle could answer, Deirdre, who was a much quicker study than Billy, noticed PhaPha's painting on the wall. "Is this the famous painting?" When Annabelle nodded, she continued, "What's it doing here?"

Instead of answering, Annabelle gestured Deirdre down the hall to Donnie's bedroom. When she returned, the former bad-ass biker chick was so pale her skin looked translucent. "I don't understand this at all. Really creepy. Whose house is this anyway? And whose dog?"

Annabelle answered the dog question first. "The dog is mine."

Deirdre looked as if she just didn't have enough energy to question what Annabelle's dog was doing on a bed beneath a PhaPha shrine in this blue house.

Annabelle continued with a question of her own. "Do you remember Donnie Bingham? From high school? This is his house."

Deirdre looked surprised, but said, "Yeah, he was in my class. Well, in my grade. He was never in class with any of us; they kept him in the back. Wait a minute. He and Phayla were friends—sort of. And, oh God, he's the butcher at Food World, right?"

Billy, who had been swinging his nine iron and muttering to himself, turned at that nugget of information and raged, "My God! Why didn't anybody think to look into this? Who else but the butcher at Food World would lay somebody out in a deli case? What's wrong with the idiot who runs the police department in this shitty little town?" He was actually spitting.

Deirdre seemed to be more offended by Billy's pejorative remark about Buster than Annabelle. Maybe J.B. was right and there *was* something going on there.

Deirdre jumped in Billy's face with, "What makes you think somebody else couldn't have killed her and then took her to Food World to make it look like Donnie did it? Maybe somebody who knew about Donnie's obsession with Phayla? Or what about the guy who was found dead out in the woods by Phayla's car? He was most likely the strangler. Or, for all I know, *you* killed both of them, Phayla and her latest boyfriend. Maybe Donnie found her already dead."

"Or maybe you killed them *yourself*, DeeDee." While Deirdre's face was still pale, Billy's was almost purple. "You always hated Phayla. You never even came to our wedding." Billy tried to pull off hurt with that last remark but failed.

"I wasn't *invited* to your wedding."

The two siblings-in-law continued hurling accusations of perceived slights and alleged wrongs, an enterprise that reminded Annabelle of when her kids were teenagers. There was nothing like a family fight to liven things up, nothing quite as vicious. Billy and Deirdre's verbal warfare gave Annabelle a minute to think, and when she did, she wondered why she wasn't getting the hell out of there. It might be hard to wake up Charlie from his mid-morning nap on Donnie's bed, but she could probably manage it. This would be the best time to leave and get Buster while Billy was pointing his golf club at Deirdre and not at her. But something made her want to stay and that something was probably just pure nosiness. She was as bad as the women at the Kwik Mart. She knew if she got Buster involved he would just kick them all out of Donnie's house and take over the investigation himself. He was bad about stuff like that.

She did need a good story to tell Buster later when he would be sure to ask why she didn't get out of Donnie's house as soon as possible after she discovered the evidence. That's when she decided she would go to her grave swearing that, before she could get away and do the right thing, the whole enterprise turned into a hostage situation with Billy Franklin holding her prisoner with his nine iron. The more she thought about it, the more confident she was that her assessment was correct and there was no escape. She'd be lucky just to survive.

Full House

In the midst of Deirdre and Billy's haranguing and Annabelle's flight of fancy, the doorbell rang. It seemed that Deirdre, not having been raised in a barn, had closed the door when she arrived. All three trespassers stopped what they were doing and just looked at each other as the bell continued to ring. So much for Billy's big talk about killing Donnie with his golf club. He looked fairly nervous and was checking out the back door. Annabelle, on the other hand, had the presence of mind to look out of the front window. Lo and behold, behind the truck, the Mercedes, and the Harley now stood a BMW that looked very much like J.B.'s.

"That's just J.B. Let her in." Annabelle didn't stop to wonder how J.B. knew she was there.

"Who's J.B.?" Billy and Deirdre asked in unison.

"My next door neighbor. The one you called my 'girl', remember, Billy?"

Billy managed to look chagrined as he contemplated his swinish behavior but still asked with some derision, "What is *she* doing here?"

"I don't know. Why don't we open the door and ask her? Besides, one *could* ask what any of *us* are doing here." Annabelle was already heading for the door, anxious to apprise J.B. on all that the morning had wrought.

"Well, J.B, this certainly is a surprise!" Annabelle attempted to look hospitable, like she had any business at all playing hostess in Donnie Bingham's house. Too bad she didn't have a fancy apron.

J.B. was the epitome of spring fashion, from the top of her newly coiffed hair to the tip of her lacquered toenails. She had on white Capri pants and a fuchsia-colored blouse that perfectly matched her fuchsia-colored strappy sandals. The woman sure could dress. However, the effect was somewhat compromised by the look of utter astonishment on her face, accentuated by her wide-open mouth. She couldn't seem to find a way to close it long enough to even begin asking the questions that would be necessary to make sense of this.

Annabelle escorted J.B. into the living room and sat her down on Donnie's plastic-covered couch, introducing her to Deirdre and trying to keep her away from Billy. It turned out that J.B. had been on her way home from Food World when she noticed the motorcade parked across the street from Donnie's house. Donnie's door was the fifth one she'd knocked on.

As soon as she sat down, J.B. started bitching about how hot it was in there and how the plastic was sticking to the back of her legs and how she wanted to wrap that golf club around Billy's stupid neck.

Annabelle said, "J.B., if you'll just shut up for a minute I'll make all of this worth your while. Look up at the painting on the wall over there."

J.B. did appear to forget about the heat and the plastic as Annabelle spun her tale, beginning with the chinaberries and ending with the hostage situation, which J.B. seemed to consider without any real seriousness.

After Annabelle finished, J.B. said, "I just have one request."

Annabelle figured J.B. was going to take the high road, and attempt to get them all to leave Donnie Bingham's house and go find Buster. Just as she was about to try to talk J.B. into staying a little bit longer in case anything else interesting happened, J.B. said, "Air conditioning. If we're gonna be hanging around this place, I got to have some cool in here." No wonder Annabelle loved J.B. so much.

As Annabelle went to turn on the window air conditioner in Donnie's living room, she didn't feel particularly guilty about trespassing in his house or violating his privacy. However, being a tightwad herself, she did feel bad about upping his electric bill. But it was important to stay cool in a hostage situation, so she proceeded to make it happen.

As Annabelle bent over to push the 'on' button on the window unit, it seemed that Donnie had yet another visitor, an additional player in the drama being performed without its main character. Peering myopically in the window of the ultramarine blue house was none other than Eula Eubanks, ace crime reporter for The Southern Sentinel. Across the street, Eula's 1987 Ford Fairlane 500, with its magnetic "Press" sign attached to the door, was parked at the end of the growing daisy chain of automotive disparity that was embellishing Donnie Bingham's street.

Donnie's Special Marinade Recipe

"Who the hell is *that* and what the hell is *she* doing here?" Billy seemed to be stuck for something novel to say as he continued to work with his golf club at what looked to be a severe slice. Annabelle couldn't tell if he was nuts or just committed to improving his game.

"Eula Eubanks. She works for the local paper. This can't be good. Wonder how she found out about this." Annabelle just stood there looking back through the window at Eula. "I guess we better let her in."

When Annabelle opened the front door, Eula looked around the room and asked, "Annabelle McGee, what on earth are you doing in Donnie Bingham's house and who are all these people?" Eula was a born reporter.

"You mean you aren't here for the scoop?" Annabelle stepped back to let Eula in.

"No, I'm meeting Donnie here to get his Special Marinade Recipe. I'm going to run it in next week's 'Gritz 'n Gravy' column."

"You mean Donnie's on his way home? I thought he worked until 5."

"He's on his lunch hour."

At that information, J.B. perked up and said in a helpful manner, "Yeah, I heard him say something about clocking out when I was placing my order for George's tenderloin."

Not to be out-snooped, Eula said, "Annabelle, you never answered my question about what you and these people are doing here."

After a quick huddle, Billy, Annabelle, Deirdre, and J.B. decided the only course would be to let Eula in on what they'd learned, since, otherwise, they felt sure she'd run to Buster.

Annabelle and J.B. escorted the latest hostage to Donnie's bedroom and, before long, Eula was seated with Deirdre, Annabelle, and J.B. in the living room. They'd run out of plastic-covered couch space and had brought in a chair from the kitchen. If it hadn't been for Billy maniacally swinging his nine iron and muttering something about titanium shafts, and if they'd had bibles and cookies in their laps, it would've looked like the Tuesday morning Methodist Ladies Circle Meeting.

"All I've got to say is I don't believe for a minute that Donnie Bingham killed anybody," Eula said with some authority. "Anybody who can make a marinade as good as Donnie's just couldn't do something ugly like that." Eula's eyes were sincere behind her harlequin-shaped glasses, which were so out of style they were back in. She pulled a small notebook out of her purse and began writing.

Annabelle added, "We need to talk about how we're going to handle Donnie when he gets home. Billy, there's no need for you to threaten him with that golf club. It'll just get him all pissed off and make you look stupid. Let's just talk to him and see if we can find out what he knows. I don't think anybody's thought to question him."

Annabelle would later wonder why she got so caught up in what happened that day in Donnie Bingham's blue house, and why she didn't do the smart thing and go find Buster. She would ultimately decide that, like Patty Hurst, she'd gotten involved in a victim mentality of some kind where she'd had to identify with her captor in order to survive. After all, Billy Franklin *was* holding them all hostage with his titanium-shafted nine iron.

CHAPTER 16

Lunch Time

The doorbell rang and Deirdre ran to answer it, not stopping to think that Donnie probably wouldn't ring the bell at his own house. The intervention committee, as Annabelle had decided to call the group trespassing on Donnie's property when she forgot to call it a hostage situation, had ultimately decided to let Deirdre talk to Donnie since she was a pastoral counselor and had experience with felons. This accord was drawn only after much discussion. While all had agreed that jumping up and yelling "Surprise!" when Donnie showed up was not a good idea, the committee wasn't unanimous in its decision to let Deirdre handle things, since Billy still wanted to beat Donnie's ass with his nine iron.

When a ready Deirdre opened the door, a Pizza Hut delivery boy was standing there with two large pizzas and a liter bottle of Diet Coke. "Pizza delivery for J.B. Jones," he announced as he unzipped his stay-warm pouch.

All eyes turned to J.B. as she held up her cell phone and said, "I was hungry and it *is* lunch time. I ordered enough for everybody." With that happy news, everyone cheered up as J.B. paid the pizza boy and he left (the single hostage to escape). The only complaints were from Billy, who didn't drink Diet Coke and Eula, who didn't like black olives. Deirdre said nothing but pulled the pepperoni off of her one small slice.

Annabelle worried a little about why Charlie hadn't come around to check out the pizza smells so, after carefully washing the poisonous chinaberry juice off of her hands, she went back to Donnie's bedroom to verify her dog's continued good health and give him Deirdre's leftover crust. He did look worn out from his morning of sleuthing but managed to raise his head enough to eat the crust without having to get up. Only a small smear of tomato sauce ended up on the ultramarine bedspread.

As she sat back down on the couch and picked up a big slice of supreme pizza, Annabelle surveyed the room and took in what appeared to be a slightly off-kilter family reunion. Billy with his Tommy Hilfiger, J.B. with her strappy sandals, Eula with her harlequin eyeglasses, Deirdre with her tattoo, and Annabelle, herself, with her chinaberry juice-stained P.E. shorts, were all sitting around congenially eating a picnic lunch in a purloined house, talking like the old friends that most of them weren't.

The committee members were so engrossed in their noon repast and their plans to be humane in helping Donnie through his confession (all except Billy, who'd mentioned some kind of torture having to do with a remote control) they didn't see the unsuspecting home owner open his back door and enter his kitchen. In fact, they didn't notice him at all until he appeared in his living room, holding a McDonald's Happy Meal and a large strawberry milkshake.

Crazy Love

Poor Donnie. He was so undone by the throng in his living room he dropped his milkshake, spattering pink on the shag carpet, and turned to run. He'd left his souped-up 1979 Chevy Malibu parked in front of his house and had walked around to the back, checking on his day lilies, without noticing either the entourage of vehicles parked across the street or the pizza smell emanating from inside. Although he was outnumbered, he figured his car could outrun anything driven by *this* group. (That's because he hadn't seen the Harley.) However, before he could make it to either of his doors, Deirdre caught up with him and went into pastor mode.

"Donnie, I know this is a shock but we're all here to help you." She tried to stand between Donnie and Billy, who was exuding malevolence. "Do you remember me? I'm Phayla's sister, Deirdre...DeeDee." A look of recognition appeared on Donnie's frightened face, so Deirdre continued. "We know about your friendship with Phayla and don't think for a minute you had a thing to do with her death. We just want to know what happened, how you got the painting, how Phayla ended up at Food World."

At this, Donnie's face collapsed as he broke down and started sobbing. Annabelle hopped up off the couch so he could sit down and she could stand next to Billy and his golf club in case he decided to use it. J.B. jumped up too, looking like she didn't want to be caught in any titanium crossfire.

"I loved her," Donnie cried into his little McDonald's napkin. "Sh-sh-she was my friend."

He blew his nose and looked up at Deirdre, who coaxed him on with soothing words. "Donnie, just tell us what happened on the day that Phayla died." Eula was just a-writin' away in her little notebook.

Donnie sat back on his couch and closed his eyes for a second as if to gather his thoughts and steel himself for what was coming next. If he'd been more savvy or enlightened, which he wasn't because he'd received his entire education in the back rooms, Donnie would've refused to answer without an attorney or at least someone from law enforcement. All he had was this vigilante posse, the members of which had already evidenced scurrilous disregard for the law, not to mention appalling manners, before he ever encountered them eating pizza in his living room.

However, when Donnie opened his eyes and started talking, he looked relieved, as if he were purging himself of something rank, something that had made him sick like a Butterball gone bad.

"PhaPha came to see me on that day. She always tried to come see me when she came to River's End. We knew each other for a long, long time. PhaPha said I was the only person who really loved her." Annabelle cast a glance at Billy to see how he was taking that comment. Although his jaw seemed to be in a spasm situation, he kept quiet, intent on Donnie's story, golf club in "at ease" position.

Donnie continued, either ignoring the fact of Billy's presence or maybe not knowing who he was. "PhaPha had sent me pictures for a long, long time. I started saving pictures of PhaPha when I was in high school. Do you remember, I helped out with the yearbook? They let me do errands and clean up. I stole some of PhaPha's pictures. She had so many. That wasn't very honest of me but I did it anyway." It seemed that Donnie was the most honest person in the room in spite of the fact that he might have killed somebody. "When PhaPha found out I liked pictures of her, she started giving them to me. She gave me pictures for a long, long time."

"On that day, PhaPha came by and brought me a new picture. It was her with a bunch of other pretty ladies all dressed up. But none of them was as pretty as PhaPha." His eyes glistened with new tears. Annabelle could just see PhaPha propping up her self-esteem with poor Donnie's adoration.

"She told me she was going to meet one of her boyfriends out in the woods near the highway. I hated it when she did things like that. I worried about her. She told me this boyfriend was mean and I asked her why she'd have a mean boyfriend. She said that she liked them mean." Donnie looked so sad at that revelation.

"So, this time I followed her. I'd never done that before but she'd never said her boyfriend was mean before. I wanted to make her safe. She'd told me there was a map drawn on the back of some painting she'd left for the boyfriend... a painting, not a picture... and he was going to meet her where the map said. I asked her why she didn't just tell him where to meet her; it'd be easier that way. She said it was more exciting her way. PhaPha liked excitement; she said that." He stopped and cleared his dry throat. "So, anyway, I followed her, or tried to. She'd sort of told me where it was. I kinda think she wanted me to follow her but I kept losing her. I finally had to follow tracks on a dirt road and it turned out to be the right place. I did a good job following her. But I was too late."

With that heartbreaking statement, a collective sigh could be heard in Donnie's living room.

Laid Out in State

In a quiet voice, Deirdre urged Donnie to continue. He took a sip of the water J.B. had brought him from the kitchen, and did as he was told.

"When I got to her, she was laying on the ground and she was dead. My beautiful Phayla was dead." Donnie's anguish was echoed by Billy at this point. Billy's face crumpled as he gripped his nine iron as if it were a lifeline. Maybe it was.

"I went over to her and she wasn't breathing. She looked like she'd been strangled because her neck had big red finger marks on it; the marks looked like sausages. I didn't know what to do. I couldn't leave her there in the woods. Wild animals mighta gotten her. Then I thought of my pretty deli case. I knew dead people had to be kept cold or they'd start to rot, like meat. I didn't want that to happen to PhaPha. Then I thought about how famous people like queens are what they call laid out in state or something like that and I thought that was what I could do for my queen. The two things I loved most in this life was Phayla and my job at Food World. I thought they ought to be together."

Everyone in the room was moved by the homage that had been paid by this simple man to Phayla Eberhart, homage that she certainly didn't deserve, unless one considered her swinish and bovinish crypt companions.

A minute or so passed before Deirdre asked her next question. "Donnie, what about Phayla's boyfriend? Did you not see him with her?"

With that question, Donnie's demeanor changed and he closed up shop in the confession department. "I don't know nothing about that." He began unwrapping his cheeseburger.

Deirdre looked around the room with an expression that said, "Uh oh, here we go." "Donnie, you have to know, or at least suspect, that he killed Phayla. Did you do anything to try to save her? Did you get there in time to try to protect her? Did you shoot Phayla's boyfriend? Is that why you didn't say anything to anybody?" Dierdre's next professional iteration would have to be law. She was really good at this. Too bad her interrogation was wrong, both legally and morally, and wouldn't hold up in court.

"I told you I don't know nothing about that." Donnie had a look on his face that indicated he wasn't about to take part in any conversation about the demise of Phayla's last boyfriend.

There was a short lull in the action as each thespian in the script being played out in Donnie Bingham's living room took a minute to personally assess plot and character development. Deirdre was attempting to figure out how to get Donnie to open up about the smelly guy. Eula seemed to be going back over her notes, and J.B. looked like she'd just remembered some ice cream melting in her car. Annabelle was worried that Charlie might be sick (or poisoned) because he wasn't investigating Donnie's cheeseburger, and Donnie was busy trying to get started on his lunch so he wouldn't have to go back to work hungry. He seemed to have a good appetite now that he'd expunged himself of info and angst. Billy, on the other hand, appeared to be in some sort of catatonic state after hearing Donnie's story.

Because the hostages were involved in their own thoughts and activities, their own inner struggle or lack thereof, they understandably missed still another visitor to the ultramarine house in River's End on that spring day. Martha Mason, like Donnie, had entered from the kitchen door after walking around the side of the house.

When she finally noticed Martha, Annabelle looked out the front window and, sure enough, there was her bicycle parked (and chained) behind Donnie's Malibu. Annabelle then turned to Eula Eubanks, who, for some reason, was taking notes as fast as her fingers could write, still sitting in her chair from the kitchen.

When Annabelle returned her attention to Martha, it seemed that Eula's productivity was well grounded and on the mark. Martha, unlike Donnie, hadn't brought her lunch in an attempt to grab a quick midday bite. She hadn't stopped to do a bike-through at McDonald's before peddling on to Donnie's blue house. Something other than sustenance was on Martha's mind.

Instead of a Happy Meal or a Fillet-O-Fish, Martha was holding in her small, trembling hands something else entirely. What she was holding was a very large, seemingly very heavy, exceedingly bona fide-looking, police-issue-like revolver, a revolver that she was attempting to point at the group as Eula, true professional that she was, continued writing.

CHAPTER 17

An Unrepentant Shooter

On Martha's hands were latex gloves and in her ears were Annabelle's wing nut dangles. Martha had done enough work with fingerprints to know how to avoid them and had enough fashion sense to know not to wear her diamond studs with her work clothes.

"Donnie, don't you say one thing. We've got this pact, remember?"

The group sitting in Donnie's living room should have been more concerned that a gun was being pointed at them collectively. However, they weren't really all that experienced at hostage situations and weren't very good at doing interventions. Plus, this was Martha Mason here. Martha didn't have the intelligence to place a complicated order at Krispy Chik, much less plan and carry out a felony. So, naiveté, instead of absence of good judgment, would have to be blamed for the hostages not jumping up, screaming bloody murder, and running from the blue house that spring day in River's End.

In that same vein, Deirdre, still standing in front of Donnie, turned to Martha and offered, with no small amount of misguided assurance, "Donnie's already told us about Phayla's death. What do *you* know about it? What pact do you have with Donnie?"

"You told! We agreed not to tell!" Martha hollered at poor Donnie, who looked like he just wanted to take his lunch back to work with him, no problem. "I can't believe you told. We'd agreed that I wouldn't tell about you putting that woman in the deli case if you wouldn't tell about me trying to kill her and hitting that man instead."

Deirdre was still in her lawyer mode and asked, continuing to avoid any deep thinking about repercussions or gunshot wounds, "You mean you killed Phayla's boyfriend? But why?" What Deirdre should've been asking was something like, "How about putting down that gun, nice and easy? Aren't we all friends here?" Apparently Deirdre didn't think to do that.

Realizing she'd made a confession of sorts and since she was the one with the gun, Martha decided to own up, her thin arms wobbling under the weight of her firearm. "I didn't mean to kill the boyfriend. I meant to kill that woman." Wobble, wobble. "She had a hold over my man. I never could understand it. She wasn't nearly as pretty as me." With that, Martha took one gloved hand off the gun in order to pat her hair, causing a deep dip in the arc of danger.

Emboldened and still not thinking to ask about the gun, Deirdre continued with, "But how were you even there? Did you follow Donnie in your car?"

"I don't own a car. I ride my bike everywhere. It's good for my figure and for the air quality." Martha managed a smug, physically fit and environmentally-conscious look in spite of the gun and the gloves and the entire ludicrous situation. "No, I hid out in the back of Donnie's car. He didn't even know I was there. He'd told me that woman was going to come see him that afternoon so I'd gone to his house to kill her. I was just sick of her and her prissy butt. Donnie would've married me a long time ago if it hadn't been for her." She continued, "I didn't get the chance to kill her, though, because she was leaving when I got there and I wasn't about to shoot her in the middle of River's End in broad daylight. I got in the back seat when Donnie went back in the house to get a Mountain Dew."

Deirdre again. "So what happened when you got to the woods?"

Martha appeared to be enjoying the attention and the respect the gun seemed to be affording her. "I got to them first. Donnie had gone over to a tree to take a pee or something, so I sneaked out of the car and I saw them having sex. Least that's what I thought they were doing. Donnie told me later the man must've been strangling her. I guess I don't know the difference. Anyway, if I'd known he was killing her I could've saved a bullet and a lot of worry."

At this point Annabelle jumped in, wanting to give Martha an out. "Martha, are you sure you weren't trying to save Phayla's life and you shot that man in an attempt to stop him from hurting her?"

"Nope, I was trying to shoot her and I missed."

A Real Man

For some reason at this point, Billy emerged from his catatonic state and decided this was the time to assert his alpha-male status in the hierarchy of the group, to be the man he was meant to be, and said to Martha, "Lady, you are fucking nuts and need to be institutionalized. My wife never did anything to you. She didn't even know you existed. She wouldn't have." Billy was using that contemptuous, condescending Southern tone that, while absolutely lacking in charm, was so much a part of who he was. Even so, it was certainly a stupid time to employ that particular affectation. Donnie, who was sitting on the couch with his burger and fries still intact, looked miserable and hungry.

Martha turned to Billy and pointed her gun at him, intuitively grasping his masculine artifice. "Don't use bad words to me. Real men don't use porn or bad words. If you were a real man, your wife wouldn't have been hanging around my man." At that point, Martha seemed to decide to take Billy's real manhood to task for not keeping PhaPha at home. Straightening her shoulders to regain control of the gun, she said, "I think I'll just shoot you in the pecker, you peckerwood pretty boy." With that, she righted the revolver one more time and pointed it somewhere in the general area of Billy's crotch, which served to make everyone in the room gasp, especially Billy.

The Hero

Just as chaos was ensuing in the plastic-covered living room of Donnie Bingham's ultramarine blue house, Charlie woke up from his nap, scratched once, shook off two times, and made his way to find Annabelle. He was hungry and something smelled good.

Joining the teeming horde, Charlie had on his party face, ready for more pizza or maybe that cheeseburger over there. All he had to do was get past the lady who was in his way.

Charlie just barely brushed up against Martha, sort of from behind. Just to move her, not to scare her or anything. Well, if the truth be known, a cold-nose strategy *was* included for insurance. Just up the back of her skirt.

Martha appeared to take exception to Charlie's ploy to get her to move out of his direct path to the cheeseburger and toppled over, screaming something about being afraid of and allergic to big dogs. In the midst of it all, the gun went off, the bullet ricocheting off the titanium shaft of Billy's nine iron (for golf aficionados, pinging off his Ping), just missing Eula Eubanks who was still taking notes in her spiral pad. That Martha was a better shot than previously thought.

The intervention committee wasn't handling this aspect of the proceeding very well as disorder proliferated and confusion abounded. Billy kept looking at his nine iron, trying to figure out what happened. Deirdre had apparently moved from lawyer mode to preacher mode and seemed to be in some kind of prayer state. Annabelle and J.B. screamed, then hugged each other and talked in unison about wetting their pants. Eula kept on writing.

When the metaphorical smoke cleared and the pandemonium abated, Buster had arrived in the nick of time and was cuffing

Martha Mason, apologizing profusely all the while. Thinking things just might be getting out of hand, J.B. had called the police department on her cell phone when she'd gone in the kitchen earlier to get Donnie's water. It had taken Buster a while to get the message since Martha wasn't at her usual station by the phone.

When Annabelle thought to look for Charlie, she was surprised not to find him whining and shaking next to her as she'd expected, since he was deathly afraid of loud noises. Instead, he was sitting on top of Donnie Bingham, sniffing the pockets of the butcher's apron he still wore. The cheeseburger was gone.

Charlie

HEY MAM, THE SCHNITZELS WOKE ME UP. THEY SMELLED SO GOOD! I SAW THE MAN WHO SMELLED SO GOOD THAT DAY. THAT MAN WHO HAD THE UGLY PICTURE. THE MAN WHO LOOKED LIKE MR. JEROME, ONLY NOT BROWN. I'M SORRY ABOUT KNOCKING THAT LADY OVER. WHAT WAS THAT LOUD NOISE? IT SCARED ME.

The Committee Adjourns

As Buster was gently handing Martha over to one of his two deputies, Annabelle heard him ask her how she'd known about the people hanging out in Donnie's house. Her answer had something to do with one of Donnie's neighbors calling the station and reporting that a well-dressed but suspicious-looking black woman was going up and down the street ringing doorbells and knocking on doors.

After taking statements from each of them, Buster busted up the intervention committee, as Annabelle had known he would. He asked Donnie to come in for further questioning and told the rest of them to go home, emphatically explaining to Billy that home meant Tallahassee. He asked Deirdre to stay and talk with him for a few minutes, looking relieved that she wasn't a murderer. That little interchange certainly seemed suspicious to Annabelle, so she mentioned it to J.B. as they took a minute to clean up the milkshake ooze and pizza trash in Donnie's living room and turn down the air conditioning. No need to cool an empty house.

As Annabelle, J.B., and Charlie were leaving, Buster's other deputy was busy directing traffic. Between the large number of vehicles parked on both sides of the street, Martha Mason being escorted out in handcuffs, and the steady procession of River's End populace driving by to see the spectacle, there was a real jam.

As they parted ways under the old chinaberry tree, J.B. said reflectively, "You know, River's End really needs its own movie theater. There just isn't enough to do in this town." Annabelle wasn't sure whether she was referring to the rubberneckers currently impeding traffic flow or to the group that had spent almost an entire spring day holed up Donnie Bingham's blue house without his permission.

CHAPTER 18

Six Months Later

Out in front of The Artful Dodger, the leaves were dancing in the November wind, finally resting in a yard that probably wouldn't be raked, at least not for a while. Even though North Georgia was the region of the state known for its autumnal metamorphosis, River's End had done itself proud this year, its maples and big old oaks wearing bonnets of burnt orange and bright yellow. The chinaberry trees were full of ripe berries waiting to be picked so someone could string them, cook them, paint them, and then sell them at the Baptist November Bazaar alongside her wing nut line.

That someone was not going to be Annabelle McGee, who had moved on to other creative and prostitutional pursuits. As she sat at her sewing machine working on plaid-shirt and striped-sweater pillows to sell during the Christmas rush, J.B. entered without knocking.

J.B. was done up in Fabulous Fallwear, with corduroy slacks and a coffee-colored sweater that beautifully matched her mocha skin tones. Annabelle was wearing old blue jeans, pink socks and the "anonymous was a woman" t-shirt one of her kids had given her for her birthday years ago. Although the shirt was faded, the message was still clear.

It had been a good summer and fall. George had made full professor and was no longer working such long hours. J.B. had taken on some lucrative clients as her web page design reputation grew, and was thinking of adding additional office space to her Victorian. Annabelle's kids were all planning to descend upon River's End some time during the holidays, and she had some new ideas for making towel racks out of old fence posts to go along with the line of tie-died towels she was thinking of creating. Best of all, her hair had grown out some. Even Stella and Charlie had had a good couple of months, on top of things from under Annabelle's covers.

"So, how was dinner with Buster last night?"

"Good. I made that pot roast thing where you throw a chuck roast, some potatoes, some carrots, and a package of onion soup mix in tin foil and then you smear a can of cream of mushroom soup over it and cook it for a couple of hours. And I had banana pudding for dessert. You know the one with instant pudding, vanilla wafers and Cool Whip? And, oh yeah, bananas."

"Sounds yummy. What did you find out?"

"What? You aren't interested in my recipes?"

"Damn it, Annabelle, tell me what you found out about Martha and Donnie and Phayla and the smelly guy."

"Can you believe it's taken this long for the judicial system to do its job? I'm so surprised. And talk about lack of information. I heard Eula Eubanks agreed to hold her story until after the trial. There was some kind of gag order."

"And?"

"Okay, okay, here goes." Once Annabelle got started, she talked for quite a while, making J.B. help her stuff pillows as she went along. J.B. kept complaining about her manicure and the musty smell of Annabelle's second-hand fabrics.

It turned out that Martha Mason had been sentenced to twenty years for trying to kill PhaPha, and missing but hitting the smelly guy. (Nobody seemed to care that she'd almost shot off Billy Franklin's pecker. They probably thought he deserved at least that for being such an ass.) Martha could've gotten off with a lesser sentence but was adamant about her guilt. Buster had said she could get parole in about seven or eight years with good behavior. Annabelle and J.B. agreed that the Georgia penitentiary system would probably be sick of Martha in a maximum of five and she'd be free as a bird and back to answering the phone and handling forensics at the River's End Police Department. They also agreed it was too bad Annabelle was no longer in the jewelry-making business since they figured she might be able to build a solid (not to mention captive) clientele at the state pen after the inmates saw Martha's wing nut dangles.

"What about Donnie?"

"He was found innocent."

"Because of his low I.Q.?"

"No, because of his butterflied pork chops. I think the judge was a fan. Plus, the state's case just might have been a little teeny bit compromised because of our intervention thing." Annabelle offered a contrite moue.

"Oops." A pause while J.B. retrieved more fiberfill. "Well, okay, what about the letter you got from Alabama, the one we all thought was from Deirdre."

"From Martha. Apparently she rode the bus to her sister's house somewhere in South Alabama and mailed the letter from there."

"What about the fact that the back door of Food World was jimmied open? Surely Donnie had a key."

"Donnie said he jimmied the lock so no one would suspect him. When asked about it, it was reported that Donnie said, with all seriousness, 'What do you think I am, stupid?'" Annabelle and J.B. stopped for minute to gain control. Neither dared to laugh at Donnie's comment as God would surely strike them dead.

"What about PhaPha's Atrocity? How did Donnie end up with it?"

"Apparently when Donnie and Martha were leaving the scene of the crime, they looked in both PhaPha's and the smelly guy's car to make sure there wasn't any evidence they were leaving behind. Somehow, the painting ended up at the police station with Martha, which was not a good thing. At some point, Donnie went to the station and picked it up, wanting to keep it as part of his PhaPha collection. He also took the gun Martha used and hid it in his cookie jar. It seems Martha was in charge of firearms at the police department, so nobody missed it. Tight ship, huh?"

"Okay, the smelly guy. Can you believe we never even knew his name? That's kind of sad." J.B. didn't look all that disheartened.

"Not really. He was a pretty bad guy. They think he was trying, at the end there, to blackmail PhaPha into giving him a large sum of money, and I don't think he was talking about the kind with John Belushi's face on it. Apparently she didn't get off on that particular scenario, so he killed her." Annabelle tucked a strand of hair behind her ear, happy to have one long enough, and continued, "The surprise is that something like this didn't happen to PhaPha sooner, what with those weird sexual games. It goes to show, just because people have money and looks, it doesn't mean they aren't screwed up."

"Speaking of screwed up rich people, what's Billy Franklin up to these days, as if I care?"

"According to Buster, he's dating some thirty-year-old news anchor for one of the television stations in Tallahassee. I think he's just happy his golf club saved his manhood. Not the first time that's happened, I'm sure."

"Are you disappointed that nothing came of that sick little relationship you two had going there for a while? I've been afraid to ask." J.B. still wasn't sure nothing had happened between Annabelle and Billy that night after Everett Pipp brought her home in his Peugeot.

"God, no. I'm relieved," Annabelle confessed truthfully. "Billy Franklin was the last thing I needed in this particular midlife crisis." With that, Annabelle remembered one last tidbit Buster had shared as he'd spooned up banana pudding seconds the night before. "Speaking of sick relationships, it seems that Donnie and Martha are to be married in a prison ceremony within the next couple of months." As both Annabelle and J.B. suppressed a giggle, she added. "He should be safe for a while since I doubt if they allow conjugal rights. I'm not really all that sure about his sex drive."

J.B. added, "I wonder if Martha will make him get rid of his photo gallery."

Annabelle stopped sewing for a minute and said, "Okay, your turn. Have you heard anything about your friend, Everett Pipp? I've been meaning to ask you about him."

J.B. had the grace to look embarrassed and admitted that Everett Pipp and Eula Eubanks were an item, apparently united by a love for Thai cooking and old cars, not to mention Mother's blessings. It seemed they'd met when Eula was sent to do an article about Mother's collection of woks from around the world.

"Dumped for Eula Eubanks. What a world. What a world." Annabelle tried to look heartbroken.

"Okay, talking about being dumped. I have to ask about Buster and Deirdre. Are they really seeing each other?"

"Yeah, it looks that way. He's been to Birmingham twice and says she's had him on both a Harley and a vegetarian diet. No wonder he ate so much of that roast last night. He was probably having tremors."

"So, what you think about that, sistuh friend?" asked J.B., using her ghetto ploy to ease the situation. She wasn't all that sure about Annabelle's feelings for her ex.

"About Buster having tremors?"

"No, you fool. About Buster hanging out with Deirdre."

"I don't have a problem with it. In fact, I'm happy to have somebody to share Buster with. He's too much for me to worry about by myself. But I do hate to admit I was wrong."

"About Deirdre being a lesbian?"

"No, about Deirdre having good taste."

With that, J.B. got up to go before Annabelle could get started about Charlie being a hero, about his good nose and his better instincts, about how he'd seemed to know Donnie was involved in some way in PhaPha's death. As she made the strange crossing from Annabelle's domain, from the tacky house with the peeling shutters and the crazy quilt of a leaf-strewn yard to her own province, to the symmetry of a perfectly-laid brick sidewalk leading to her handsome and historically-correct domicile, J.B. continued to ponder the Charlie question.

As she opened her door and headed to the order that was her state-of-the-art computer with its high-speed cable connection, J.B. came to the same conclusion as always, the only one that seemed reasonable when she was out of Annabelle range. It just had to have been a big coincidence.

It was obvious to everyone, except Annabelle, that Charlie, for all of his sweetness, was just a dumb animal, incapable of constructive thought or follow through. There was no way Charlie could have had anything at all to do with solving the mystery of who killed Phayla Eberhart. To consider otherwise would be to accept some kind of parallel universe, a place bigger than the World Wide Web, a road longer than the information superhighway, a cosmos where intuition superceded cognition, a reality based on something other than common sense and good taste.

"Bullshit," said J.B., as she booted up.

Charlie and Stella

HEY CAT, I WISH MAM WOULD GO SEE THE SCHNITZEL MAN AGAIN AND BRING ME SOMETHING GOOD TO EAT. I'M TIRED OF JUST CAT FOOD. THE SCHNITZEL MAN LOOKS LIKE MR. JEROME, ONLY NOT BROWN.

Will you quit obsessing about the damned schnitzel man? I'm sick of it. I thought dogs were supposed to color blind. Now move over, you're sitting on my tail.

LaVergne, TN USA
16 December 2009
167162LV00001B/83/A